EMP LODGE

Dark Retreat

Dark Hunt

Dark Defiance

Dark Destruction

Dark Redemption

Dark Revival

DARK DEFIANCE

EMP LODGE SERIES BOOK THREE

BY GRACE HAMILTON

Blurb

Strength in numbers can make the difference between life and death—but only the right numbers.

Megan Wolford has finally found herself a family she and her young daughter can rely on in terrifying times. Their group is small, but they trust each other with their lives—and day by day, Wyatt is showing her how to love again. With a long winter looming, they'll have to hunker down in the lodge to survive, but there are deadlier threats to their safety than harsh conditions.

When a neighboring group is struck by ruthless raiders led by the fearsome Connor McDaniels, they must form an uneasy alliance with Megan's new family. She doesn't take kindly to newcomers, but they will need every pair of hands they can get to fight off the raiders. After McDaniels turns his sights on Megan's people, she plans an assault that will put an end to the threat he poses once and for all—she'll need every person she can get at her side. But she has to learn to trust them first.

Thank you for purchasing 'Dark Defiance'

(EMP Lodge Series Book Three)

Get prepared and sign-up to my mailing list

to be notified of my next release!

Sign up here: www.GraceHamiltonBooks.com/mailing-list/

You can also follow me on Facebook

fb.me/AuthorGraceHamilton

Table of Contents

Chapter One

Megan Wolford stared through the trees, desperate to find her. Jack was right by her side, which was a place he'd tended to frequent in the past month. With Wyatt not totally healed from stepping in the bear trap—forced to hobble around in the walking boot Greg had given her and use Albert's crutches—Megan and Jack had taken on many of his responsibilities. Together, they had become a formidable team.

"Do you see her?" Megan asked.

"No," Jack said. The frustration in his voice mimicked Megan's own feeling.

"Where in the world could she have gotten off to?"

Megan was tired of scouring the woods looking for her, but they couldn't leave without her.

"It probably took off, deeper into the forest this time now that it's more familiar with the area."

"Her," Megan corrected, not trying to hide her irritation.

Evan and Bryan tramped through the trees behind them, making their frustration clear with the amount of noise they were making. Bryan was shaking his head. "I say let it come back when it's ready."

"Her!" Megan shouted.

She stomped away from the three men. They were heartless threatening to leave her out here. She knew Jack would never do that. He had become one of her closest friends and he would never do anything that would hurt Megan like that.

Wyatt and Jack were not only brothers, but best friends. Wyatt trusted Jack with his life. Megan trusted Wyatt's judgment and had naturally gravitated towards a friendship with his brother. She wasn't the best at making new friends but she had started to consider Jack her closest companion by default.

He was one of the nicest, kindest men she had ever met. She was so thankful she had gotten the chance to know him. Their relationship had evolved into one you could compare to a sister and brother bond.

Evan and Bryan went in the opposite direction, knowing Megan wouldn't give up.

Jack caught up with Megan and they fell into an easy stride, walking side by side.

"She couldn't have gotten far.," he reassured her. "I hope."

Evan's baritone voice boomed through the trees to the left.

"Over here! Hurry up, Megan! I'm not even going to try to catch her. It's up to you."

Megan and Jack took off running through the trees. Stepping on a small rock, she twisted her ankle, pain shooting up her shin all the way to the hip.

"Ow!" She stopped and leaned against a tree.

Her ankle had healed, but every so often she managed to turn just right and it stretched the weak muscles and healing tendons.

Sucking in a deep breath, she took a minute to breathe through the pain.

"That's it," Jack said, putting a hand on her shoulder. "Just breathe. It will pass."

Megan closed her eyes and nodded. Jack was the brother she never had and would have always wanted. He pushed her when she needed it, but was always there to give her a few kind words when things were especially tough.

Wyatt had a lot on his plate with his injury. He was used to leading the family, he'd been especially grumpy and touchy these last few weeks. She knew it was because he felt bad that he couldn't do as much to help prep for winter.

She completely understood the feeling. Been there, done that, she thought.

Jack stood beside her while Megan leaned against the tree, waiting for the pain to pass. He was a patient man and had helped her through many situations just like this one. Jack and Megan had been forced to do most the hunting and scavenging with Wyatt down. Chase generally stayed around the lodge to act as head of security, with Brenda and Albert rotating watch shifts.

It was an effective system. Everyone was on edge at the lodge, waiting for retaliation after the incident at Brenda's house. Brenda had remained at the lodge as a permanent resident, which Megan wasn't sure if it was a good thing or not. She wanted to trust the woman, but it wasn't something that came naturally to her. It didn't help that Brenda was a difficult person to get to know. She didn't say a lot and when she did, it was nothing personal. Megan knew very little about the woman who had ultimately saved Caitlin's life.

This trip was supposed to be Jack and Megan's last before the snow started to fall. They were going to be scavenging what was left of the town with Evan and Bryan. When Evan had radioed Albert, asking if they wanted to go along on the last trip, it was Wyatt who agreed that it would be a good idea. He was feeling better and had insisted Chase go along to help carry supplies back. They needed to pad their stores before winter. The trip was risky, but Megan had agreed with Wyatt and they'd managed to score big on their trip into town. She couldn't wait to get back to the lodge to show Wyatt the haul they had found and the surprise gift she received from Evan.

Brenda had volunteered to go with them, but Megan convinced her to stay at the lodge. With Chase going, Brenda was needed for security purposes. Their numbers were spread thin with Wyatt down. Everyone had to do a little more to help make up for his inability to do anything strenuous.

"It is going to kill one of us one of these days," Jack said, trying to get a laugh out of Megan.

"You're right. If I don't kill her first," Megan grumbled.

They both knew she would never do anything to bring the little thing harm, but she certainly did try Megan's patience.

"You ready? Let's go before it, I mean she, takes off again."

Megan stuck close behind Jack as they ran as fast as possible through the wooded area. She could hear Evan and Bryan shouting ahead. All that would do is scare her and she would run off again. Megan was going to explain, again, how to calm the poor thing down.

When they finally reached the clearing where Evan and Bryan were making a huge fuss, Megan had to hold back a laugh. Both men looked frantic. They were waving their arms in the air, dodging back and forth, as the baby goat bleated in glee and slipped between Bryan's legs.

Megan and Jack watched as the men came up with the plan to divide and conquer. It was decided Evan would capture the doeling, who watched him closely while Bryan served as backup should she run away again. After a moment of hesitation, Evan dove for the goat but she easily moved out of the way. Unable to stop his forward momentum, Evan hit the ground with a loud thump, chest first.

They all laughed. Except Evan, who came slowly to his knees taking painful breaths.

"Megan, I am about sick of that stupid goat. You need to put her on a leash or something," he huffed out, standing and brushing himself off.

"It's a baby, Evan. You don't chain up a baby goat," she chastised.

Megan walked towards the doeling, who was playfully butting her head against a small tree stump. The kid was occupied, allowing Megan to walk right up to her.

It was a game they had played many times in the past few days. The little doeling was far more precocious than her brother, who tended to stick around the pen and didn't try too hard to get out. The same could not be said for his sister, who constantly escaped and ran off, enjoying the merry chase that ensued.

Megan looked at the stump that had caught little Misty's attention. Only now, upon closer inspection, she could see it wasn't a tree stump. It was a cross made from tree branches.

She took a step back with Misty in her arms, now realizing where she stood. There were eight crosses.

Megan couldn't stop the chill that shivered down her spine.

Chapter Two

Megan dropped to her knees, keeping one hand on Misty. The crosses didn't have names, but some of the mounds they sat on had little bouquets of wildflowers laid on top of the dirt. Megan looked at the sad scene and thought about all the loss Evan's group had recently endured.

The Raiders were stepping up their game. They had become more violent and aggressive with each new attack. These eight crosses represented the people murdered without rhyme or reason at the hands of the rampaging men. Megan had seen how evil they were firsthand, and couldn't imagine what the people buried under each of the crosses had endured.

The other three came to stand beside her. It was a moment of silence the dead all deserved. The people lying in this makeshift cemetery were heroes.

Evan knelt at one of the crosses, his face contorted with pain. These were people he had come to love.

"I'm so sorry, I couldn't protect you," he whispered. "I am going to do everything I can to protect your mother and sister."

Megan didn't have to ask who was buried in the plot. The Hot Wheels in the dirt was enough. It was a heart wrenching scene. Megan couldn't imagine how much pain Evan was in. She knew he felt responsible for the deaths of the people who had come to live in his camp. The four of them stayed for a minute longer, each paying their respects. Jack took Misty from Megan.

"You're sticking with me, little lady. You keep running off and a big, bad wolf is going to eat you alive."

Megan punched his shoulder, "Don't say that to her. She doesn't know any better."

Jack laughed, but it was forced. They all wanted to get away from the crosses and the sadness they awakened. Evan brought up the rear, though he was still pale-faced from sight.

Megan didn't know what to say to help him feel better so she chose not to say anything at all. Grief was a tricky business. It was too easy to say the wrong thing and make the emotions harder. Instead, she focused on Misty, softly breathing in Jack's arms.

"Hey, sweet, baby girl. You are such a naughty goat. One of these times something is going to eat you before I can save you," she said in a baby voice, rubbing the goat's hard head.

Jack rolled his eyes, "It isn't a baby. It's a menace."

"Stop it. She is the cutest little girl ever and likes to play."

Bryan snorted from behind. "You have a weird idea of cute."

Megan waited to see if Evan would join in or if he was still lost in his grief but he spoke up.

"I hope for your sake, Megan, that thing doesn't have you chasing it all over the mountain this winter. Wyatt won't be happy to run around trying to save you all the time."

Megan laughed. Evan was so right. While she chased the goat, Wyatt would be chasing her. The vision had them all laughing, dispelling the darkness that had been hanging over them a moment ago. Death was hitting a little too close to home for all of them. It was like a menacing cloud, waiting and watching. Always hanging over them, no matter what they did.

Megan was tired of the fear. Tired of always wondering if today was the day The Raiders or some other violent gang would decide to kill them.

They walked back into Evan's camp, the tents they used for newcomers as well as a decoy against potential marauders looking the worse for wear. The cabin they had helped put the roof on was now in use along with the guard cabin. Unfortunately, his group was much smaller than it had been a month ago, and the people who were once primed to make a new life for themselves seemed to be going about their chores without any sense of real purpose.

Megan watched as little Amy stood next to her mom. Tara was staring off into space, her shoulders slumped forward. Evan immediately walked to her and wrapped his arms around her. The woman appeared so fragile—so different than when Megan was here last.

The scene was difficult to accept. Chase was chopping wood, with another young man. They stacked the split logs in a neat row next to the newest cabin. When Misty had run off, he refused to go looking for her—again.

"Jack, put her in the pen with little Mason," Megan instructed.

The pen was nothing more than some wood pallets held together with rope. It was not built to hold a goat intent on running free, but Megan wasn't too worried about it. They would be leaving soon and they would build something much stronger at the lodge. She made a mental note to make sure the fence was nice and high. Building a pen for the goats had not been on the agenda so soon, but she couldn't pass up the opportunity or deny the gift Evan had so generously given.

Tara walked to the gazebo, pulling out a large dish from the oven. Megan could smell the fresh garlic and oregano from here. It smelled heavenly. Fresh herbs were always a real treat. The plan was to eat dinner together and then head out first thing in the morning.

"It sure is getting cold, huh?" Jack asked, standing next to her.

Megan rubbed her hands together, "It sure is. I hope we're going to be okay this winter. I remember years ago, we had a bad one in Spokane. There was so much snow on the ground, the plows basically gave up. We had some friends who lived up in the mountains and they had to dig their way out from the front door, there was so much snow."

Jack whistled, "Yep. I imagine we are in for something similar. I'm not nervous, though. We've been preparing for this winter for close to a year."

Megan knew he only said the words to reassure her. No one was feeling confident going into this winter. They had been fortunate so far. There had been a light dusting of snow, but it was typically gone within a few hours.

Bryan was standing close by, watching the goats play in the pen. "Most of us are from Oregon near the coast. We're not used to snow in general. This winter is going to be a tough time for us for sure. I just hope we're ready."

"You will do just fine," Megan assured him. "It's all about having plenty of firewood, food, water and preparing to spend a lot of time inside."

"I hope we have enough," Bryan said. "By our best guesstimate, we've cut more than eight cords. Do you think it will be enough?"

Megan shrugged, "Possibly. It's always best to have too much and not need it than to need it and not have enough. Even if you don't use all the wood this winter, you'll still need it come spring."

Bryan nodded in agreement.

"I'm going to see if Tara needs help with dinner. Jack, did you give her that meat before we went chasing after Misty?"

He nodded, "Yep, and she promised to make something that would knock our socks off."

Megan laughed as they joined Tara. "Is there anything I can do?" she asked her.

"You can help me get the dishes. We have them stashed in the guard cabin."

"Great," Megan said following her towards the tiny cabin.

When they got back to the gazebo, Chase, Evan and Jack were seated at the table. Megan heard them talking about the different types of wood they were stacking on the pile.

"Avoid burning that pine, especially at night," Chase instructed. "It burns fast and hot, which is great for heating up a cold cabin, but it will be out before you know it."

"Got it," Evan said. "Stick with the fir and birch."

Jack added his two cents, "The red fir is the best. Birch is very hard and can be a bit of a pain to get going. Do what you can to split it into smaller pieces. We like to add it to the fire once we have the stove and chimney heated and there are some nice hot coals to keep it going. The bark on the birch logs will ignite immediately, which can also help a sluggish fire."

"Good to know. Thanks guys. This is stuff we should know, but, well, we just don't have the experience."

Megan imagined that if she hadn't found the Morris family, she would be in the same predicament. These people had little experience with harsh mountain winters. They were struggling to get enough food stored and with the Raiders stealing their supplies, it was seriously threatening their ability to survive the winter.

"So, how is Wyatt doing?" Bryan asked, sitting down next to Chase.

"He's good," Jack responded. "He's not in the best of moods right now. My brother makes for a terrible patient and doesn't like to be laid up."

Megan defended the man she loved, "Hey now. He's only a little grumpy and only when he can't come on trips like this. He hates being down."

"Is his leg any better?" Evan asked.

Jack nodded, "Thankfully, yes, but it still gives him some problems if he overdoes it. Then he has to deal with my mom and this one," he said using his thumb to gesture to Megan.

She rolled her eyes. "I didn't see him making it easy on me

when I was supposed to be resting my ankle."

They all laughed. Each of them had witnessed Wyatt doting on her and his demands that she not do anything at all. He had been a real mother hen.

"I think we're ready to eat," Tara announced. "Amy, go tell the others dinner is ready."

They ate the meal quickly. The sun had already set, dropping the temperature and making it too cold to sit around in the gazebo.

"We better head to bed," Jack announced. "We need to get an early start in the morning."

Megan checked the goats one more time. They were fast asleep in the little shelter they had inside the pen. She hoped they would stay put through the night.

Jack stood outside their shared tent.

"All good?"

"Yep, hopefully she doesn't get any wild ideas about going for a midnight stroll."

From inside the tent, she could hear Chase grumbling about how cold it was. Bryan brought them a couple extra blankets.

"I'm real sorry about this. I know it's cold. Pretty soon we won't be able to use these tents."

"It's okay, man," Jack assured him. "We'll be fine. You get some rest and if we don't see you in the morning, take care and thanks for taking us into town. This portable HAM radio and solar panel is more than we could have expected to find. I can't wait to come back this spring and do some more digging down there."

Bryan nodded, "Yeah, we've had some pretty good finds there lately. Good luck with your goats, too. Hopefully they don't give you too many problems."

Megan smiled, "Thank you so much for the goats. It's the best surprise I've had in a really long time."

"Well, the old guy had far more goats than he needed. I think he was actually relieved to get rid of them before winter."

"We're happy to have them. It'll give us a jumpstart on the whole milk and cheese thing. Just think, by next winter we'll be trading cheese!"

She was so excited to show her daughter, Caitlin, and Ryland the baby goats. She knew Wyatt would be thrilled, but not nearly as much as his mom, Rosie, and his sister-in-law, Willow. Albert would feign nonchalance, but she knew he was a softy when it came to animals and she suspected he would dote on them more than anyone else.

They were such characters. The goats would provide plenty of entertainment throughout the long, boring winter to come.

"Good night, guys," Bryan said, walking to the small cabin.

Chapter Three

Megan's eyes popped open. It was dark inside the tent. She blinked a few times and tried to clear the cobwebs from her brain. Something had awoken her. She laid perfectly still, listening to Jack and Chase breathing deep.

There! It was a noise outside the tent. She couldn't tell what it was. Was it anything? Maybe it was Misty. The goat had probably jumped over the fence wall and was milling about the camp.

She could hear the change in Jack's breathing and knew he was now awake as well.

"What is it?" she whispered.

"I don't know," he whispered back. "Shh," he said, slowly sitting up.

Chase sat up silently and slipped out of his sleeping bag.

Megan wasn't about to stay in the tent while they went out to investigate. She had seen the horror movies. The person who stayed behind always ended up murdered in some gruesome way. Not her. No way.

The three of them knelt at the opening of the tent, waiting in silence for another noise beyond the flimsy walls of their tent.

Megan clapped her hand over her mouth to muffle the

involuntary gasp.

There were men's voices and heavy footsteps just outside the tent.

She looked to Jack, waiting for him to assure her it was just Evan or Bryan milling about.

The look on his face told her all she needed to know.

Megan didn't hesitate and reached back under the blankets to grab their weapons. They had decided never to be unarmed again. They each tucked a handgun into the back of their waistbands, pulling their shirts over the top to conceal the weapon.

If they could get through a confrontation without pulling their guns, they would. Firearms would only escalate things and someone would likely end up shot and probably killed. In this new world, with hospitals and antibiotics a thing of the past, a bullet wound was hard to survive. Even an untreated cut from a rusty piece of metal or a bad case of the flu could kill you.

Chase held up a finger and silently counted off three.

Megan took a deep breath and followed the two men out through the flap. That is, she tried to crawl out. Jack was standing in front of the tent door, keeping her inside. She jabbed the back of his leg, trying to tell him to move.

He dropped his left hand down and gestured for her to get back.

Oh this can't be good, she thought to herself.

Jack should know by now she didn't like playing the damsel in distress or the little lady who needed saving. She would wait and see what his plan was before she threw a fit. She may be the one that had to save them and that would require her presence to be a surprise.

She knelt, ready to spring, waiting for the signal.

It didn't come right away. While Megan waited, she looked around for something to hold her hair back. She had Rosie cut off quite a bit of the length off, but it still got in her way. She found Jack's ball cap in the corner of the tent.

Grabbing it, she tucked her hair up under it before pulling it tightly on her head

"What can we do for you gentleman?" Chase asked. The words were polite. His tone of voice revealed he was anything but nice.

"Oh, I think you know."

The voice wasn't familiar. Megan could hear laughter from several men. She knew instinctively that this had to be the Raiders. They were back to steal and cause more trouble. She clenched her fists. These men were some of the worst of humanity taking what little people had with no thought to their survival.

A grunt followed by, "Who the hell are you?"

Megan tensed. The man was walking closer to Jack and Chase.

"You guys took all the extra supplies we had last time," Bryan's voice came from the side of the tent. "We have nothing more for you to take."

It was then Megan realized it was barking dogs that had first alerted her to the intruders. They must have woken Bryan as well. That meant the rest of the camp would hear the commotion. She silently hoped they stayed out of sight. She couldn't deal with any more deaths.

"I'll decide if you have anything I want. We're looking for some friends of ours," the gruff voice said, right outside the tent door.

Jack's hand came down again. He wanted her to stay inside.

"I doubt we've seen any friends of yours," Jack stated with a large dose of sarcasm.

"OOMPH!"

"You better step back!" Chase shouted.

Megan saw Jack's legs buckle. The man had just hit him! She wanted to burst through the tent door, firing her gun at everyone in view.

Jack must have known what she was thinking and wagged his

hand back and forth.

"I think maybe you have seen our friends. We are looking for a group of little ladies. We seem to keep missing them. One's real cute. Long hair and has a little girl. The other one is some wannabe soldier. Short hair, big glasses," he said, describing Brenda.

"As we told you the last two times you've been through, we haven't seen the women you described," Bryan said, trying to hide the irritation in his voice.

Megan was shaking with anger. These men were worse than bullies and Jack, Chase and Bryan were at their mercy. She had no idea how many men were out there. Could they fight back if they had to? The thought of a gun battle at close range scared her to death.

"Whoa, dude. No need to shoot anymore people. Take what you can find and go. We have nothing left," Bryan started. "These two just happened on our camp. We don't know them and quite frankly, they aren't welcome. We don't have the resources to support any more people."

Chase backed up Bryan's claim, "We're looking for somewhere to live through the winter. We don't want any trouble."

There was a moment of silence. Megan hoped that meant the

bad guys bought their story and would just go away.

BOOM!

A gunshot rang out followed by what sounded like a yip from a dog. Megan held back a scream. The opening in the tent was completely blocked. All she could see were feet and calves. She stared at Jack's legs, waiting to see if he would collapse. When he remained standing, she waited for screaming. Anything to tell her who had just been shot.

"That was not called for!" Chase yelled.

"This time it was a dog. Next time it will be you," the man said. "Or maybe I'll shoot one of those goats."

Another gunshot rang out and Megan saw red. Jack's hand immediately popped down. She was about ready to rip that hand off.

"I'm taking what I want. Move." The voice was right outside the tent, now.

Megan froze. He was coming in.

Within seconds Jack's legs disappeared from her view and were replaced by a large, full-bodied man. When he popped his head in the tent, she flinched.

The man was ugly. Not ugly. Hideous. His scraggly beard and orange-tinted hair were a mess. In the center of his face was a bulbous nose that spread across his face. The redness on his nose and cheeks indicated he was a heavy drinker. She knew the telltale signs.

"Well, what do we have here?" he snarled, revealing a set of yellow teeth.

"Stay away from me," Megan said with as much authority as she could muster.

The tent was far too small to fit them both.

"Leave her alone," Jack said, pushing the man out of the way.

He extended his hand to Megan. She gladly took it and crawled out of the tent. The pungent odor coming off the man as she went by him nearly made her gag. He refused to move, forcing her to brush her body up against his.

He smiled making her skin crawl.

The man stood up and looked Megan up and down. She prayed he wouldn't recognize her as one of the women he had just described. With her new haircut tucked inside the hat, she hoped it was enough to disguise her appearance.

Jack put his arm around her and pulled her in close effectively staking his claim.

The man crossed his arms over his large belly, "She's yours?"

Chase and Jack exchanged a look. Megan nearly choked when

24

Chase responded.

"Ours."

That got a laugh out of all the men.

"Well shoot. You two certainly don't look the type, but her," he said eyeing Megan again. "She does."

Megan was offended, but Jack squeezed her, signaling her to bite her tongue.

"McDaniels," shouted one of the men who had gone to the new cabin. "Got some stuff. Looks like they just restocked."

Bryan started to move towards the cabin, but Chase held him back, "Let it go, man. It isn't worth your life."

Megan frantically looked around the area. A dog lay dead on the ground about twenty feet away, blood pooling around its body. She quickly looked to the goat pen and saw her kids playing like there was nothing to worry about.

"Thank God," she said under her breath.

Jack squeezed his arm around her. "They're fine."

"Load up what you can," the man, who Megan figured out was McDaniels, ordered.

"So, miss," he looked at her again. "Have you seen the three lovely ladies that have managed to escape us?"

There were angry shouts and nasty words from the men at the mention of the three women.

Megan shook her head no.

McDaniels squinted and cocked his head slightly, "If you three just got here, where'd you come from?"

Chase casually stepped forward, effectively shielding Jack as he took the opportunity to slyly push Megan behind him.

On any other day, she would take offense at being shoved behind a man. It was something Wyatt always did and it usually annoyed her. Not today. She didn't want that man to look at her and figure out who she was.

When they didn't answer, he pulled out the gun and aimed it at Megan's goats.

Megan jabbed Jack in the back so hard he was pushed into Chase.

"We've been wandering around. No real direction," Chase stated.

McDaniels put the gun back in the holster at his waist.

"Maybe this will help," he said pulling out a map from his back pocket. He unfolded it, holding it out for Chase to look at. "This is where we lost our friends," he said the last word with a sneer.

Megan moved around Jack and Chase to see the map.

She saw the area where Brenda's house was located. Her eyes were drawn to an area of the map that had a large red circle on it. She turned to look at Jack who gave a very subtle, almost imperceptible nod of the head.

She looked at the map again. The circled area was not far from Evan's camp. She could see small x's on the map. There was an x on Brenda's house and on Evan's camp. Megan had to play it cool. The x's marked camps that had been raided. It would make sense the red circle was where the Raiders were holing up. It could also indicate a stash of supplies. Maybe the red circle was a target? Megan made a mental note on the location. Once Wyatt was healed, she wanted to check out the area. It could be a warehouse full of goods.

"We haven't seen a thing the whole time we've been walking all over this stupid mountain," she said, trying to sound as dimwitted as possible.

McDaniels stepped forward, eyeing her with intensity. Megan's heart was racing under the scrutiny. She prayed he wouldn't ask her to remove the hat. "I wasn't asking you, little lady. I was asking your boyfriends here."

Chase and Jack both confirmed Megan's story.

"We haven't seen anything or anyone. We're hoping to find

shelter. These guys don't want us around so we planned on leaving at first light."

McDaniels slowly folded the map back up, put it in his pocket and drew the gun again, pointing it at Misty who was on her hind legs, peering over the fence.

Megan lurched forward, prepared to tackle him, but Jack held her back.

McDaniels held the gun on Misty another second before putting it back in the holster.

He turned back to Megan, Jack and Chase.

"You're lying. I know there are plenty of groups around this mountain. Do you know why I know? Because I already found them and killed plenty of them for lying to me."

They didn't bother defending their lie. There was no point. Megan was terrified anything they said at this point would unleash his anger. Would he open fire, killing them where they stood? Her instinct was to shout at the injustice, but common sense told her to keep her mouth shut.

"Move out of the way, so I can see what you got hiding in that tent," he said, shoving Chase to the side.

It only took him a few minutes to emerge, carrying the new ball Megan had found in town. She had planned on giving it to Ryland and Caitlin. They'd become obsessed with playing catch.

She glared at him, but didn't say a word. He would probably shoot her or the goats if she tried to argue.

The other men had finished searching the other tents and the two smaller cabins. Each of them was carrying their finds, laughing and joking about what they'd managed to steal.

"You all take care now," McDaniels said before turning and walking out of the camp.

Once they were out of sight, Megan turned to Jack and Chase, hands on her hips.

"How did they know to look for us?"

Bryan stepped forward, "We're pretty sure they always leave a scout behind. Someone as a lookout."

A chill ran down her spine. With the gunfight at Brenda's house and the four dead Raiders, they'd assumed Megan had taken everyone out, but now it sounded like there must have been at least one more hiding among the trees. It was a scary thought. If Chase and Jack hadn't arrived when they did, reinforcements could have arrived and killed them all. She knew without a doubt they would have been killed where they stood.

"Why did we just let them take everything? Why is nobody taking these guys out? This is ridiculous!"

When no one answered, she looked at all the people standing around, staring into the trees where the men had disappeared with their food for the winter and other items.

"They're going to keep coming back! Don't you see that?" she shouted in frustration.

It wasn't in her simply to lie down and be walked all over. Not anymore. Not ever again. Not since Kyle had tried to kill her and her daughter.

It was Bryan who spoke for the entire group.

"We can't take them. They will kill each and every one of us. If they don't kill us, there is a chance they would take the survivors as prisoners. Would you risk your daughter or Jack's wife being held captive by those men?"

That's when Megan realized what they were truly up against. Evan and Bryan's group had been diminished to the point they couldn't fight back. They were at McDaniels' mercy.

A thought flashed through her mind. Strength in numbers. She quickly pushed it out of her thoughts. Strength in numbers also meant more people to trust, and Megan wasn't ready to invite anyone else into the group right now.

Chapter Four

Jack pulled Megan away from the others.

"We can invite them to come back with us," he whispered.

"Jack, we can't. We don't know these people well enough and we don't have enough food or shelter for them."

"Megan, you need to think about how much help and strength they would bring. We're struggling to get everything done."

"No, Jack."

She tugged at his arm but he turned and walked back to where the others were standing.

"Why don't you and your people come back to the lodge? We can work something out as far as where you can all stay but it isn't safe for you here anymore. Those guys are going to be back. You know it and I know it," Jack stated firmly.

Jack clearly didn't buy into Megan's apprehensions about bringing more people home. He was like a kid finding stray animals to adopt. She was going to have a discussion with him about his tendency to trust so openly.

On top of that, their own food supplies were dwindling with use and despite conservation efforts; she didn't think there would be enough, which meant hunting in the snow. Rosie and Willow had been collecting herbs to help against various ailments but they would run out quickly if that many people were living in such tight quarters and someone got sick. They would all be sure to get it. Clothing, bedding, wood for heat and cooking, the list of things they needed to survive the winter was endless and would be rapidly depleted with so many extra bodies making for crowded sleeping arrangements.

It had taken her months to trust Wyatt, Jack, and the rest of the group with whom she lived. Inviting this group into their happy home would disrupt everything. Megan knew she would always be second-guessing the newcomers' motives. Would they be safe to have around her daughter?

In the end, it was Caitlin's safety that was her number one priority and always would be. If she didn't feel like she could trust the people Jack planned on bringing in, she would have to leave. It was that simple.

Megan nearly wept with joy when Evan turned Jack down.

Thank God!

"Thanks, Jack, really, but we can't accept."

Bryan was a little more vehement in his own refusal.

"We aren't going to let them run us out of the homes we built with our own two hands. We've made a life here. We'll fight them when we're stronger."

Megan wanted to hug him. Now, that very difficult conversation she was going to have with Jack could wait.

Her elation quickly faded when she looked around the camp at the faces of those who were left behind. They were exhausted. The remaining children looked anxious. Megan noticed Amy clinging to her mom.

There was another little boy who also seemed nervous almost all the time. Last night at dinner, he had nearly jumped out of his seat when a strong gust of wind blew a plate to the ground, smashing it to pieces.

It was hard not to notice the faces that were missing as well. Their numbers had been depleted, but it was more than just a missing face. The ones who had been killed were someone's loved ones.

Her heart went out to them, but she had to think about her own daughter and her family. It pained her to be so selfish, but it was the way the world was nowadays. She certainly didn't create it or make it that way. It was people like McDaniels and Kyle Grice that were destroying any bit of humanity that remained in this dark world.

Jack and Chase helped dig a hole to bury the dog before heading out. It gave Megan the chance to pack up their things after McDaniels thoroughly tossed their packs. The portable HAM radio and folding solar panel were ignored.

The man was, clearly, pure evil. He took the ball, knowing it was probably something special, but left the real valuables behind. Megan knew he was bad news and prayed he didn't find his way to the lodge. McDaniels and his crew could easily overpower them at the lodge. They didn't have Evan's manpower or numbers had been easily defeated.

She pushed the thought out of her mind. There was no point in stressing over something she couldn't prevent or change.

"You ready?" Jack asked poking his head inside the tent.

"Yep. Let's get out of here."

Chase was standing outside, trying his best to keep the goats from dragging him into the trees. Megan wanted to burst out laughing, but instead walked over and took the leashes from him. It was crude, but it would work so long as they didn't decide to chew through the ropes.

The three of them talked very little as they hurried back to the lodge. They all had a sense of urgency about them. They didn't have to say the words.

With McDaniels' Raiders in the area, they were all terrified the violent men would find the lodge when it was sorely unmanned and unprotected.

As they approached the perimeter of the property, it was Chase who stated the obvious.

"We are so unprepared. This flimsy fence and these silly booby traps are not going to stop the likes of McDaniels."

Megan looked up, expecting to find Albert in the bird's nest, but he was nowhere to be found.

"I thought you told them to stay on guard?" Megan asked Chase. He was the security expert and instrumental in setting up warning systems around the property to alert them in the event they had company and that included someone being on watch.

Obviously, his advice had been ignored.

As the three of them moved past the perimeter and closer to the lodge, it became painfully obvious they were extremely vulnerable. They weren't trying to conceal their presence or avoid traps. They didn't have to, because there weren't any. It was an eye opener.

"We have to change this," Chase stated.

He didn't need to state what this was. They all knew. After seeing what had happened at Evan's camp and the ruthless nature of McDaniels, it was painfully clear they needed to change their ways. The mountain wasn't safe anymore.

Despite living in peace and harmony with the other groups that had made homes all over the mountain for months, McDaniels was destroying that serenity. There was no point in moping about it. It was simply time to act.

Megan heard a small scream and knew instantly it was from Caitlin.

Jack looked at her, gauging her reaction.

Megan kept walking.

"Do you want to run?" Jack asked.

"Nope. Not going to risk twisting my ankle."

He looked at her as if she had lost her mind.

"That was a scream of joy, Jack. I'm not heartless, but I am not going to save the day when she is obviously playing with Duke or Ryland."

Another scream of glee.

Megan raised an eyebrow.

"Okay, now I can hear the laughter."

When the lodge came into sight, there was a sense of relief to see it still standing, but there was also some frustration.

"We could have walked right up to the lodge and they wouldn't have a clue," Chase said with irritation.

The defenses they had up weren't enough. Their focus had been more of an early warning system. They had fences and they were prepared to fight should intruders breach the perimeter, but Megan wanted to set more traps and obstacles that would prevent them from even needing to fight. She thought back to the medieval ages when castles had moats. They needed that kind of a defense system.

Megan took a second to take in the sight before her.

Wyatt, Ryland and Caitlin were all outside playing catch. It had been their favorite pastime the past few weeks, which is why she had so wanted to bring them a new ball. McDaniels had ruined her surprise.

"Hey!" Wyatt said when he noticed them watching.

Caitlin screamed again when she saw the baby goats they were carrying.

"How'd it go?" Wyatt asked as he walked closer. The surprise on his face when he saw the goats was enough to get a chuckle out of Jack.

Chase nodded his head, but didn't answer.

"What happened?" he asked. The tone was serious. Megan gave him a look that said not here, not now. He got it and focused his attention on the goats that had made instant friends with Ryland and Caitlin.

"Mom, they're so cute. I love them!"

Megan smiled, "They are cute, but they're kind of rowdy. We need to get a strong fence built to keep them home. They tend to run away."

"What are their names?" Ryland asked.

Jack knelt, rubbing the baby buck's head, "This is Mason and this little, wild girl is Misty."

Duke raced towards them. Megan realized they had no idea how he would respond to other animals.

"Stop him!" she yelled at no one.

But there was no stopping the German Shepherd. He was on a mission to investigate the newcomers.

The dog came to a screeching halt in front of the goats and started sniffing every inch of them. The goats didn't seem to notice the big, black nose violating their space and happily played with Ryland and Caitlin.

Jack had his hand out, ready to pull the dog back, just in case.

Once Duke had inspected the newcomers, he focused his attention on Megan and gleefully licked her face when she bent down. The two had become very good friends when she was laid up.

"I missed you too, big guy," Megan told him, scratching behind his ears.

"He is going to be jealous. He's claimed you and won't appreciate you paying a lot of attention to those two," Jack said gesturing to the goats.

Megan grinned as she continued to pet the dog. "He'll get over it. There's plenty of me to go around."

"You guys look exhausted. Mom saved you some dinner. Let's go in. The kids can keep an eye on the goats," Wyatt said, clearly anxious to hear what happened.

"We need to secure an area first. That goat," Chase said pointing to Misty's brown head, "Is an escape artist. We spent more time looking for and chasing her than I care to talk about."

Wyatt nodded, "You three go in, we already have that pen we were going to use for pigs. I'll just make sure it's secure."

Ryland was still carrying the baseball.

"You want me to hold that bud?" Jack asked his son.

Ryland shook his head, "Nope, I got it."

The ball had become one of the most treasured items in the lodge. The kids were both careful not to set it down somewhere and forget about it. The fact that there could have been two balls made her angry. That man was evil.

The three weary travelers walked to the mudroom they had recently built, removed their boots and stepped inside the lodge. It was warm and inviting.

Megan took a moment to breathe in the smells. She could

smell Rosie's homemade soap, which she'd taken to adding mint to after Megan's suggestion, the basil and oregano in what smelled like one of Willow's casseroles, and what smelled like burning apple wood from the fire place. Each of the smells signified home to her. The lodge was her home. The people here were her family and she loved them all, but if they didn't change their ways, everything she held dear was in jeopardy.

It was Brenda who came down the stairs to greet them.

Since coming to the lodge, she had slowly been working her way into the group. She was a huge help, but Megan still couldn't bring herself to trust her. Brenda was polite and certainly did her part around the lodge, but Megan remembered the terror she went through during those days Caitlin was hidden from her.

"Hey guys. How'd it go?"

"We did pretty well. Got a few things that will help. Didn't get any food to speak of." Jack turned and gave a mischievous look to Megan. "Unless you count Megan's goats."

Megan punched him in the arm.

"Goats? This time of year? Wow. That's great. What kind?" Brenda asked.

"Nubians," Megan responded. "They aren't for eating. They'll eventually breed and Misty will be our milk goat."

"Misty?"

"The female," Megan said with exasperation in her voice.

When Jack gave her a look, she realized she was being rude.

"I'm sorry," she quickly apologized. "It's been a long few days and I'm exhausted."

Rosie and Willow heard about the goats and had quickly rushed outside to see the adorable new additions.

Albert had been watching from the kitchen table. Once Rosie and Willow were out the door, he stood and eyed each one of them.

"So, when are we going to talk about what happened?"

Megan, Chase and Jack all exchanged a look.

"Once we get the kids settled. And yes, we do need to have a serious discussion."

Albert nodded his head, "Sit down and eat. We'll wait."

Megan was not looking forward to telling the others about the death and destruction. It was going to be a tough conversation.

Chapter Five

"Not until I know the kids are asleep," Megan said when Wyatt demanded to know what happened.

All of the adults had gathered at the table, waiting to hear about their trip.

Megan didn't want Caitlin to know what had happened at Evan's camp. The senseless murder of innocent people, including children, was a lot for anyone to handle, let alone a little girl. She couldn't shield Caitlin from all the horrible things in the world, but she could certainly try.

The adults sat around the table. Everyone appeared nervous as they waited for someone to talk.

Chase started the conversation by explaining what happened to Evan's camp and the number of dead that suffered at the hands of McDaniels and the Raiders.

Willow and Rosie silently cried as they listened to what had happened. Rosie took it harder than the rest. She had been very fond of Donavan and the many others who had been killed.

Wyatt was furious. He couldn't believe the men had killed a child. "That was a line that should never be crossed," he ground out between clenched teeth, slamming his fist into the table.

They spent a few minutes talking about the murders and the goods that were stolen.

"They don't know about the large cabin?" Wyatt asked.

Chase shook his head, "No. So far Evan and his people have managed to keep it under wraps. But I think they know it's only a matter of time."

Wyatt seethed. Megan put her hand on his leg under the table, offering support.

"Right now, they're staying in the main camp and only going to the large cabin at night. Bryan thinks McDaniels has someone watching them. It's a bad situation over there," Jack explained.

Willow was openly sobbing. Jack rubbed her back, trying to calm her down.

Rosie silently shook her head, "That poor woman."

Megan knew she was referring to Tara, Donavan's mother. The thought of losing a child was too much to bear.

"We're in bad shape when it comes to defenses here," Chase stated. "We have nothing to stop them and if they do come knocking, we don't have the numbers or the firepower to hold them back."

Willow stood up, "We need to go. We need to leave this place and go back to town. It isn't safe."

Megan was a little shocked by her outburst. Willow was always so calm but the look on her face revealed she was anything but calm. She was on the verge of panic. Her hands were shaking and her eyes darted around the room.

Megan could tell she was mentally packing and choosing what to take and what to leave.

Jack put his hand on her arm, gently pulling her back down to the table.

"Hon, everywhere we go is going to have similar groups like this. Bad guys were here before the EMP and they are going to be around now. The difference is we don't have prisons or law enforcement to control them. It's up to us."

"I don't care, Jack. I don't want to sit here day in and day out wondering if today is the day those men show up. They're looking for them," she shouted pointing to Megan and Brenda. "That guy is hell-bent on revenge. He will find us! They killed that little boy, Jack. I would die if they hurt or killed Ryland. I can't live through that!"

Willow's outburst was understandable. They all felt it, but were keeping their fear under wraps. It was terrifying. Megan thought about the kids playing ball outside. Even that was too dangerous now. The men could sneak up on them at any time.

They had to make some serious changes. They could no longer

be complacent. Their little piece of paradise at the lodge was in jeopardy.

Chase spoke up, "We have to be our own protectors. No one is going to save us, but we don't have to be victims. We have to plan and prepare to defend ourselves. We won't let them hurt the kids, Willow. I promise you that."

Willow shook her head, "Don't make a promise you can't keep, Chase."

It was Rosie who spoke next.

"Sweetie, we can't go traipsing through the wilderness in the dead of winter. That is far more dangerous than any bully. We have to trust in ourselves to protect our own."

"She's right," Wyatt confirmed. "We don't even know if we're ready to make it through winter with all the supplies we have stored away. Leaving it all behind is not an option. The weather and starvation would kill us faster than McDaniels could."

The words were harsh, but Megan knew they were meant to drive home the point. They had to step up their game. They couldn't leave the lodge with winter approaching, which would be as much of a death sentence as McDaniels finding them. They had to stay—and fight.

Megan knew Rosie and Wyatt were both thinking back to Dale's murder in their own home in the days following the EMP.

No matter where they went, there was danger.

"Why can't we go find them, sneak up on them and kill them all?" Megan didn't understand why they had to wait for an attack. Why couldn't they be the attackers?

Wyatt smiled at her, "You are a fierce woman, Megan Wolford."

She knew there was a big 'but' coming.

"But, you need to understand these guys are ruthless. We don't know how many there are. They seem to be multiplying by the day. We can't simply go in, attack and hope for the best."

Brenda quietly added, "You have to cut off the head off the snake."

Chase, Jack and Wyatt all nodded in agreement.

"Well, then we do that!" Megan said enthusiastically. It sounded like an excellent plan.

"Megan, we can't simply storm in there, because, well, first, we don't know where there is and we can't go in not knowing how many or what kind of defenses they have. It would be a suicide mission. Even one of us being killed would jeopardize the safety of everyone here."

It was Jack whose voice of reason finally made her see the light.

"We watch, we plan, and then we attack," he said with such confidence in his voice it made her feel like it would all be okay.

Willow had been quiet.

"Why don't they come here? You said we don't have the numbers or the firepower. If Evan's group is here, we have the numbers and we can find more guns."

Megan cringed. Clearly Jack and Willow thought the same way about growing their numbers here at the lodge. After his impromptu invitation back at Evan's camp and their rejection, she thought that idea had been laid to rest.

Wyatt must have felt Megan tense up. He rubbed her leg to relax her.

"It's a good idea, but I already asked and they said no," Jack said.

"Jack, you can't just go inviting everyone to live here," Albert chimed in.

Jack looked at Albert, Brenda, Chase and then Megan, "If we weren't willing to take people in, there are a few of you who wouldn't be here now."

The words stung. Megan had felt like such a part of the family, she sometimes forgot they had to make a conscious decision to allow her to stay. Albert and Chase were friends of the family. Their position in the group was only possible because of Jack and

Wyatt's willingness to accept them.

Brenda was still working to find her place.

"Jack, that's different. You're talking about inviting many people to live here when we don't know if we can support ourselves. It would more than triple our current numbers. I don't think any one of us here regrets who is here. Right?"

"I'm sorry. I didn't mean to sound callous or rude, but I think we all need to understand how vulnerable we are. Evan's group was much larger than our small number and they were easily overtaken."

Rosie smiled, "The more the merrier."

Megan laughed. She couldn't help it. She didn't share that same sentiment, but more people meant more guns aimed at the bad guys. Maybe that wasn't so bad, but the potential downside still made her hesitate.

The meeting was unofficially adjourned. They were all exhausted and they each had a lot to think about.

"What are you thinking?" Wyatt asked as they lay in bed.

"I want that man dead and I want to be the one who does it."

She knew her words shocked Wyatt. She had never been the type to wish death on anyone, let alone be the one who would inflict the damage, but this was different. This man was evil and she wanted to rid the world of his vile ways. Since the Kyle situation, Megan found she was far more willing to kill another human than she ever thought possible. Survival had a way of making a person do things they never thought they would do.

"Megan, I have no doubt in my mind that you will be the one who kills him. I don't know why, but I just know you're going to be the one who takes care of this problem. But it isn't going to be tomorrow. It isn't going to be next week. You have to be smart and methodical about this."

She was silent for several minutes. Plotting and planning how she was going to get McDaniels.

"I am going to build an army."

"What?"

"I am going to gather an army and we are going to take that man out."

Wyatt chuckled, "That's a pretty lofty goal, but I think you're on the right track."

"You'll help me?"

Wyatt leaned over and kissed her, "Damn straight, I will."

She laid there in the silence thinking about how she would gather an army.

"We need to make trips into town as soon as spring comes.

There are going to be others who are willing to stand up to those men. Every person we can recruit will strengthen our numbers. Evan can also recruit the people on the other side of the mountain."

"Do you intend to bring them here?"

"No!" she practically yelled.

"I think we go to them. Come up with a central meeting place. This way we all get to keep our close-knit groups, but we still have the help when we need it. We'll be allies. We can come up with some kind of signal we can each send out if we're in trouble."

"It's a good idea, Megan. Really good. I like how you're thinking long term and strategy. More allies mean more trading opportunities."

She started to say something more.

He put his hand on her wrist, "Babe, it isn't going to happen tonight. Tonight we need to get some sleep. I can already tell Chase is going to be making us work hard tomorrow. Relax. Go to sleep."

Megan sighed. Her mind was running at a hundred miles a minute. There was so much to plan. So much to think about. Sleep was going to be impossible. She considered getting up and pacing, but knew Wyatt would pull her back to bed.

She laid there for almost an hour. Her body felt as if she had slammed a thermos of coffee. She couldn't take it another minute and got out of bed. She quietly opened the door and walked towards the kitchen.

"Couldn't sleep?"

She froze and for a split second she thought she'd scream.

It was Jack. Through the firelight coming from the woodstove she could see him sitting at the table.

"Have a seat. There's a pot of water on the stove. I'll make some tea. My mom says this stuff is supposed to make you sleepy."

Megan sat down and waited for him to bring her tea.

They sat in silence for several minutes.

"What's on your mind?" he asked.

"I want to form an army to take out McDaniels."

Jack laughed, "Well then, will you be planning a trip to the moon afterwards?"

"Stop. I'm serious. We can do it, Jack. With all of us here and if we can get Evan and Bryan on board, we can get a group that is strong enough to us of these Raiders. We can all go back to living in peace or at least until the next bad guy comes along."

"Megan, I know you are serious and that's great. You know

we've got your back."

She sipped her tea, waiting for some magic to happen. She was still wired.

"If we kill McDaniels, we probably won't have to worry about the rest. Like Brenda said; head of the snake and all of that."

"What if someone else takes his place?" Jack questioned her.

"Then we kill that one too."

Jack whistled, "You have turned into a lean, mean, killing machine."

"You know it isn't like that, but Jack, can you even wrap your head around what would happen if they attack us here? What would happen to Ryland? Willow? Caitlin?"

He nodded, "I don't want to think about that. There is no use borrowing trouble, as my mom would say. Tomorrow, we do what we can to reinforce the perimeter and make the lodge safer. We will also go with your plan and start talking to others and building our army. All we can do is try."

"I think if we killed McDaniels, then you're right, someone will try to take his place. But, it isn't like they are some organized military faction. They don't have ranks. They will kill each other in the process. Each one of them will want to be the boss. Isn't that what happens in the mob?"

Jack laughed, "I guess so. I'm not real familiar with mob culture, but I have watched a few movies."

"I think we can focus on that horrible man, take out a few others, and they will ultimately kill themselves off and disperse."

They finished their tea in silence.

"Get some sleep, Megan. We have a busy few weeks. Don't worry about what you can't change. We will focus on what we can do and let the chips fall where they may."

Chapter Six

When Megan woke up the following morning, she knew she had slept late. The voices coming from the kitchen told her everyone else was already up and preparing for the busy day.

She let out a moan. She had not slept well at all—even with the help of the tea.

There was a gentle knock on the door before Wyatt came through.

"Hey, sleepyhead. How ya feeling?"

She groaned again in response, burying her head in the pillow.

"Well, if you would have gone to bed when I told you to," he playfully lectured.

"I know, I know. Is everyone already working?"

"Yep, Caitlin and Ryland are out with the goats. We let them out of the pen and, so far, they're sticking close to the lodge. They've found a pine tree they're enamored with for now."

"Can't we stay in bed today?" she half-joked, knowing it wasn't possible. She was already sliding out of bed, getting ready for what was likely going to be a grueling day of hard work.

"Nope. Chase has lists and lists and more lists about what we need to get done to make this place safer and better prepared.

Clearly, you weren't the only one who couldn't sleep last night."

She shook her head, "No, I guess not, but I am the only one who couldn't get out of bed this morning."

"You needed the rest. You've been pushing yourself too hard since the accident. Personally, I'm excited for the first massive snowfall that keeps us all indoors, sitting around, reading books or snuggling in bed to stay warm."

She laughed. "Oh, you are a dreamer, aren't you?"

Megan got dressed and splashed cold water on her face. Now ready to face the world. The weather had been holding, which meant she had made it a habit to dress in layers. The mornings were cool, but once they got busy and the temperature rose, she would be hot. She laced up her sturdy boots. Gone were the days when she slid into a pair of comfortable Nikes. Her footwear was all about durability and very little about comfort.

Chase and Albert had several pieces of notebook paper on the table and were each making notes on the pages. When Megan got closer she could see drawings and diagrams of the lodge. There were little chicken scratch notes on each of the pages.

Chase had been very busy.

He looked up but didn't say a word. She could see the focus in his eyes and the determination to make the lodge comparable to Fort Knox. He was committed to making the place impenetrable.

"What can I do?" Megan asked, anxious to get started.

"You, Rosie and Willow are going to work on the lodge itself. We need to make it a little less obvious from a distance. The height of the building makes it stick out like a sore thumb. We want it to blend in with the surroundings. The rest of us are going to work on the fences and setting traps. Brenda is an expert in that area, as we all know."

Brenda had been standing in the kitchen, chatting with Willow. When she first arrived, she had been a little sensitive about the traps that had injured Caitlin and Wyatt. Now, everyone was taking it more seriously.

Megan had watched Brenda come out of the shell she had been hiding in. The woman was very funny. She had a very dry sense of humor, which was common in those who were very intelligent.

"I'm gonna check on the kids. All of them I guess," Megan added when she realized the play on words. "I'll be back in a few and then we can get started," she said to Willow on her way out the door.

Megan had no idea how they were going to hide the two-story building, but she was interested to see what Chase had come up with.

Chase had followed her outside and was staring up at the massive structure. It wasn't like Brenda's tiny little house or even

Evan's larger cabin that had a thick screen of trees surrounding it. It was very big, which was great for the many people living in it, but not so great for inconspicuousness.

Megan checked on the kids. They were happily playing with the baby goats. Misty and Mason were jumping and climbing on everything they could find, including Caitlin and Ryland. All of them were having a great time. Duke was lying nearby, keeping a close watch on the activities, but didn't seem to want to join in.

"You're such a good boy, Dukey boy. You bark if things get out of control," she said, rubbing behind the dog's ears.

Megan thought about telling Caitlin to put on a heavier coat, but realized it was a bit warmer today than it had been the last few days. Every day it didn't snow was a day to be thankful.

"Be careful and stay close to the lodge," Megan warned the kids before going back to where Chase was still staring, deep in thought.

"What do you think?" she asked him.

He shook his head, "There's nothing we can do really to hide this thing. I mean, how do you hide a lodge? The rule of camouflage is to break the lines. That isn't going to be possible with a structure this size."

Megan nodded, pretending to understand, but she really didn't. "Wait, no. I don't get it. What do you mean, break the lines?"

Chase started to walk to the side of the lodge and stared up again pointing at the building.

"Because of the lodge's size and boxy shape, it stands out among the trees. What we need to do is camouflage or blur all those straight lines, which aren't normal in the wild, to make it less obvious from a distance. The logs have faded and they are technically natural to the area, so we do have that going for us. But, with the lack of trees close to the building, it doesn't conceal the place very well," Chase stated.

She could tell he was getting frustrated. Megan wanted to help, but didn't have a clue what to suggest.

"It would be different if we had months or a year to try to get this done, but we have days, maybe weeks. If anything happens, I'll be kicking myself for not insisting we do this as soon as we got here. We've been far too careless with our safety."

Jack and Wyatt had come outside and were standing in a line next to Chase. All four of them stared at the lodge.

"There is no point in wasting time trying to camouflage it, Chase. Let's just do what we can and focus our energy on keeping people from ever getting close enough to see it," Wyatt suggested.

"We have to do something. I say we have your mom and Willow plant some of the native plants around the foundation of the lodge. Over time, it will grow and climb and help conceal the walls. There are already some good starts, but it needs to be thicker. We need some of those heavy vines to climb the full height of the lodge."

Megan offered to pass along the information.

"Anything else we can do?"

Chase smiled, "I think all of us have some busy nights by the fire ahead of us. I have an idea. We need to make some camo netting. It will help conceal the lodge from those on the outskirts of the perimeter."

Jack laughed, "Do you realize how much netting that will be?"

"We only need to do the three sides for now. The backside is concealed by the hill. The main goal will be to cover those windows, which reflect the sun. I love the windows, but they are a signal to anyone who is paying attention."

"Got it," Megan said all business-like. She had no idea what it took to make a camo net, but she was on board. Whatever it took to keep the lodge family safe.

Brenda had joined the party, "We need to fortify. I did some things at my house that helped make it a little tougher to get into. Megan, you remember?

"That's a good idea."

Megan quickly explained the barricades across the doors and

the window coverings.

Chase agreed.

"Brenda, once you have given us your plan for traps around the area, why don't you jot down what we need to do to make this lodge as close to a fortress as possible."

The woman involuntarily stood at attention. Megan watched her hand start to come up. She was going to salute Chase. She must have realized what she was doing and stopped midway.

"Old habits die hard," she said with a sheepish smile.

"It's all good. I like that you're willing to help. Your experience is going to be a huge asset," Chase told her. "Jack and Wyatt, you're with me. Albert, you have guard duty."

Everyone nodded and dispersed. They all knew what to do.

Chase stopped Megan as she turned to leave, "I'll be right in to show you, Willow and Rosie how to make that netting."

Megan headed in. Chase's experience in the military and then in security services made him very qualified for the job.

Megan found Willow and Rosie upstairs. They were both sitting on a couch, facing each other. Willow looked like she hadn't slept a wink.

"How are you doing?" Megan asked her.

"Oh, a nervous wreck to be honest. I hate feeling as if we're sitting ducks. I can't seem to get my mind on anything else."

Rosie had apparently been trying to calm her, but it wasn't working. Megan decided to try herself.

"Well, Chase will be in soon. He's going to show us how to make some camo netting to help hide the lodge from a distance."

Willow and Rosie both looked at her like she had lost her mind.

Megan laughed, "Hey, I am just telling you what he told me. It's to be our chore the next few days while the rest of them work on fortifying our little castle here."

Willow stood, "Well, maybe that will help take my mind off what is surely coming our way."

She headed downstairs. Her fear and anxiety were apparent in every inch of her body language.

Once she was down the stairs, Megan turned to Rosie, "Is she going to be okay?"

Rosie shrugged, "She's worried. We all are, but she doesn't hide it quite as well as the rest of us. Hopefully these net things will keep her busy—that'll help. If she feels like she is doing something to keep her family safe, it may help relax her. Busy work is always my remedy for stress."

Megan agreed with Rosie. Sitting around and freaking out over what might or might not happen wasn't going to help anyone. They followed Willow downstairs to wait for Chase.

McDaniels was not going to keep them living in fear. She would kill him before she allowed them all to fall apart due to one man threatening them.

He didn't deserve that kind of power.

Chapter Seven

Chase strode into the lodge, carrying a large spool of paracord and looked at Megan, Willow and Rosie.

"Okay, this is going to require some space. It's probably best if we do this upstairs," he said heading up.

Megan followed him, with Willow and Rosie close behind—they were all keen to see what exactly would be done with the paracord. Chase instructed them to help him push the couches together, out of the way to make enough space on the floor to lay out lengths of cord.

"We are going to use this twine as the frame," he said, gesturing with his hands. "Measure out about ten-foot lengths. Don't make them too much bigger than that or it will be too heavy."

"What are we making exactly?" Willow asked.

"Camo nets. Sort of. But these will be like a ghillie suit. First we make the net, and then we will attach leaves, branches and other plant debris to the cordage. The nets will then be thrown over the roof to help camouflage the lodge."

Willow was the first to point out the obvious, "Ten feet isn't going to be enough."

"No, it won't, which is why we are going to need several for each side of the lodge. Once you get them constructed, we will attach the nets to the roof. Given the size of the place, it's really our only option."

"Okay, so show us what to do," Megan said, keen to get started.

Chase laid out a length of the twine. He pulled out a pocket knife and spliced the paracord, making it easier to pull the individual strands apart.

"So, each of these strands needs to be about ten to eleven feet long. Tie them to the length of twine," he demonstrated. "Tie a length of cord every eight inches or so. It doesn't have to be perfect." Each of the women grabbed a length of cord and started the process of tying the knots as Chase watched.

"Now, we need to make boxes, so we are going to put twine down both sides and across the bottom. Start on the left, tie the strand to the twine. Then, make a knot with the horizontal strand over the vertical strand." Chase demonstrated again. "Like this." He did the full row, finishing by tying the strand to the piece of twine on the right. There were squares stretching across the entire length.

"That's it. Now, go ahead and space horizontal strands down the length. The boxes don't have to be perfect. Our foliage is going to cover them so it won't matter. We just need a frame to attach the foliage."

"I think we can handle that. Right ladies?" Megan asked Willow and Rosie who were studying the beginnings of the net stretched across the ground.

"Yep, we got it. How many do we need, Chase?" Rosie asked.

"You know, the more we have, the more camouflage we can cover the lodge with. But with three sides of the lodge to cover, ideally twelve to start and we will go from there."

"Got it. Thanks, Chase," Megan said dropping to her knees to get started.

The three women got busy pulling apart the paracord and tying knots. It was tedious, but Megan could already see Willow's anxiety lessening a bit. The women were silent while they worked. They split up the work into an assembly line of sorts. Willow tied the strands on one side while Rosie and Megan each worked on taking the strand and tying it along the vertical strands.

"I think we can have the kids help us with this," Megan stated, trying to make some conversation.

Willow agreed. "And that will keep them inside so we can keep an eye on them."

Megan grimaced. She had just inadvertently fueled Willow's anxiety. She didn't want the kids to be prisoners.

With the three of them working together, they easily

completed six nets over a couple hours, which would allow them to hang two from each side of the lodge. They were just about finished with the nets and ready to start the next phase of adding foliage.

"Are you ladies okay doing this while I go out and start collecting some stuff to put on these nets?" Megan asked. She hated being cooped up inside.

The sun was actually out. Who knew how many more days they had to enjoy the sunshine and mild temperatures.

"I think we're good here," Rosie said with a smile. "You go get your fill of vitamin D!"

Megan laughed, "You caught me! I promise I will be actually working as well."

Megan grabbed a large basket and headed out the door. The glorious sunshine hit her in the face. She closed her eyes and leaned her head back, taking in a deep breath of fresh air. She took a moment to appreciate how great it felt.

"You okay?"

Jack's voice cut through her sun worshipping.

"Yes, just enjoying the feel of the sun on my face. It's so nice out here. Isn't it unseasonably warm?"

"Ya, I guess it is. Good for us so we can get all of this stuff done. You would not believe what Chase is doing. He is going full-on Rambo. Between him and Brenda, I am a little worried about walking more than twenty feet away from the lodge."

Megan laughed, "That bad, huh?"

"Yes. And then some. Where are you headed?"

"Grabbing some stuff to put on the nets we've been making."

When he looked at her with the look that said he didn't buy it, she laughed again.

"Alright, I wanted to be outside. The windows are great, but there is nothing like actually feeling the sun on your face and smelling the fresh air."

Jack agreed.

"I need to go get these supplies and head back out there before my new drill sergeant decides. I've been gone too long."

"Okay, good luck." Megan decided to go see what was going on, with the intent to gather supplies for the nets on her way back.

Megan walked to the stream, taking her time to enjoy every smell and sight she could. The kids were playing catch while the goats napped in the sunshine close by. Megan noticed Misty hadn't run off yet. Maybe it was the fence that encouraged her to jump and run. She saw a challenge and took it. The last thing they needed was a stubborn goat.

Was there any other kind? Megan thought, smiling to herself.

When she got to the stream, she could see Wyatt and Brenda on the other side. She was glad they were enclosing the stream inside the main perimeter. They needed the water supply.

Wyatt glanced up and waved her over.

"Come see what we're doing. We're booby trapping the hell out of this place."

Brenda looked at Megan and nodded. She was intent on digging with the shovel. With Wyatt's leg not completely healed, he couldn't use it.

"We are digging holes around the perimeter and placing Brenda's traps inside some of them. Slamming into a hole should slow anyone down, triggering a trap and they may well be stopped for good," he said with a grimace.

"How are we going to know where the holes are?" Megan asked, worried about the kids or even one of her goats accidentally falling in.

Wyatt picked up a white rock. They were natural in the environment, especially around the stream.

"We are placing a couple of these on either side of the hole."

Megan looked up and down the stream and spotted a few more of the rocks. To a person who didn't know, the rocks appeared random.

She didn't like the idea of it being so dangerous, but knew it was the way life was going to be until they could take care of McDaniels and his gang.

"Okay. What else?"

Wyatt smiled, "Well, follow me and I will take you to Chase. The man is a genius. Between him and Brenda they have come up with some very good defensive measures. I just pray they work."

Megan turned her head up and waved at Albert, sitting in his usual spot in the bird's nest.

Albert shouted down, "Be careful down there. They got this place more dangerous than a minefield."

"Careful!" Wyatt shouted, yanking her into him.

"Hooks," he said pointing up.

There were large fish hooks hanging from tree limbs. One more step and she would have had a hook in her face. Now, that was dangerous. And effective. The fishing line was practically transparent, making it difficult to see the trap until it was too late.

"We can't use those big hooks for fishing in the stream, so we are putting them to good use. Think of the property as a grid. The hooks are before the traps, coming from the outside. If a person gets through the hooks, they will be dealing with the traps."

"Why here?" Megan asked. "There is a lot of area to cover to completely surround the lodge."

Chase's voice cut through the silence of the forest, "This is the most obvious point of entry. It has the clearest path, which we are going to have to work on. This path is calling to people to follow it. Next year, we need to do what Evan's people did and not create paths leading directly to the lodge."

Megan nodded. They had all used this same path to the point it was a nice trail. Unfortunately, that made it easy for anyone wandering through the forest to follow it right to their front door.

"Are you surrounding the whole area with traps then?" she asked, not fully understanding.

"Yes, eventually. If we focus on this area, we're sure to take out a good majority of raiders. They're going to take the path of least resistance. But, we will also have other deterrents around the property," Chase explained.

"You need a honey pot!" Albert shouted from his spot, high in the trees.

Chase rolled his eyes, "One thing at a time old man."

"What's a honey pot?" Megan envisioned some of Rosie's precious honey sitting by the stream. It wasn't quite clicking for her.

Wyatt explained, "He means a lure or something that ensures

they come this way. The path is probably enough, but we need to put something in plain sight. To distract them."

Chase nodded, "If we had the time, I would have a small storage shed built. Put some stuff in it and let them raid it. The shed will be rigged with plenty of traps. It will attract them to one area, much like flies to honey. Then we can attack. Think of it like a roach motel. They check in, but never check out."

Megan shuddered. She had no idea she was living with people who were capable of such maniacal plots. They were all taking this very seriously, which should have made her feel better, but it only worried her more.

If Willow found out, it would probably send her into a full-blown panic attack.

Jack came back across the stream. He had one of their old backpacks on. There were lengths of wood sticking up and over his head from where he was carrying them in the pack. He was also carrying the bucket of nails they had been collecting.

"Do I even want to know?" Megan asked.

Jack smiled, "This one was my idea. I'm going to hammer these rusty nails into the wood scraps and leave them scattered about the area. We can't use the wood for building, so we'll put it to use this way. The nails and wood will be covered by grass, pine needles and brush. Anyone walking through here is going to get a big surprise. Stepping on a rusty nail will hurt like heck. If that doesn't slow them down, the infection and hopefully tetanus that follows will take them out. Assuming their boot soles aren't too thick."

"Good plan. Very smart, Jack," Megan said giving him the kudos he was looking for.

Chase grabbed the pack off Jack's back and the two of them headed further upstream to start placing the boards.

"Wyatt, I get all the defenses, but what if they get through? How are we going to know they are coming?"

"Chase wants to build more lookouts, but the problem is we don't have enough people to man them and defend the lodge."

"We need two-way radios." Megan stated.

Wyatt nodded, "We need a lot of things. We focused so much on stockpiling food and other supplies we didn't put enough attention on the actual defenses. I guess we thought the fences and alarms would be enough. None of us could have expected someone like McDaniels. We know better now."

He turned and hugged her close, "I just hope we haven't set ourselves up to be attacked. Chase isn't happy right now. He is more upset with himself for not putting enough attention on the security aspect. Those silly traps we put up to keep Kyle out are no match for McDaniels."

Megan kissed him, "We'll be okay. We have to be."

Chapter Eight

Connor McDaniels stood on the porch looking over his little compound. His men were below, standing over a fire, warming their hands. He knew they were talking about him. His leadership was on rocky ground.

They had come to this area expecting to find a lot of food and wealth. Unfortunately, things didn't turn out as planned. They had no steady food supply and with winter coming, things were not looking good. If they didn't hit a prepper house that had a stockpile, his men would turn on him. He could feel it.

Connor watched as one of them tore into a piece of jerky. The men didn't get the idea of saving and rationing. They ate and drank when they wanted, without thinking about where they would find more. These were not the kind of men who would just leave him when they decided they didn't like the way he was leading. No. They would kill him first.

He spun around when he heard a noise behind him. His right-hand man, Ben, stood in the doorway. "Should we load up?"

"Yes. What are they down there grumbling about now?"

Ben's gaze fell to the floor, as it always did when he didn't want to tell Connor the truth. Lately, it was happening a lot.

"Just tell me."

"They're hungry. They want real food. All this dried stuff is old. I'm a bit tired of it myself. Don't these people store any actual food around here?"

Connor flinched. He had led the group up to this part of the country because he knew it was ripe with preppers and survivalists. He knew for a fact just how much food and gear was up here. What he didn't realize was eating freeze-dried food day in and day out was rough.

He craved fresh meat. The freeze-dried stuff was bland and the small packages weren't enough to fill his belly. Connor couldn't imagine anyone living long-term on the stuff.

Instead of showing any kind of fear in front of Ben, he pushed back. He didn't want Ben to tell the others he wasn't as fearless and powerful as he had put on.

"You tell them sniveling brats, fresh food isn't going to be served on a platter. If they want meat, they have to actually hunt to get it. What'd you think we would find? A freezer full of casseroles and meat?"

He stepped closer to Ben, causing the other man to take a step back.

His size had been a huge advantage and he used it to intimidate those around him. His parents thought he was lazy and would never amount to anything. Look at him now. All those years hiding out in his cousin's basement had paid off.

"You tell them to get their crap together. We'll go out scouting. I know there are prepper groups all over this mountain."

"Got it, but just so you know," Ben pushed back just enough to prove he wasn't a total coward, "If we don't actually find anything, none of us plans on sticking around. This mountain ain't gonna be too friendly come this winter. We refuse to starve because our leader couldn't figure out where the good stuff was."

Connor glared at him. "You do whatever you have to do. Get the men ready."

He turned back to looking over the hillside. This house had been a great find, but if they didn't find food to stockpile soon, it wouldn't matter.

There had to be more, he just didn't know how much broader their search would have to be. These preppers were wily. His cousin had made a killing catering to these people selling all kinds of prepping gear through his website. Business had been booming and he'd managed to rope him into working for him packing up orders. Back then, they had joked about the crazy people that called themselves preppers and survivalists.

When the EMP hit and it became obvious it was a dog eat dog world, he went to where he knew the people were prepared. These northern parts of Washington, Idaho and Montana were where he shipped a lot of supplies. He had looked it up on a map to see what was so special about the area. All he could see were mountains.

That had to be the appeal. There were plenty of places to hide away from the millions of people living in the cities and suburbs. Preppers liked to be alone, which is what he was taking advantage of now. They had been raiding small homesteads and had been able to live off of the bounty of stockpiled goods.

All the preppers had thought they were so smart, living off the grid and isolating themselves. It just made it easier for guys like him to pick them off, one at a time.

Those small homesteads and cabins were no match for his men. All they had to do was threaten violence and things were handed over. In some cases, he had to make sure his point was made. Shooting someone was usually enough incentive to get them to turn over their food and water.

A man shouted out from below, "Let's go, McDaniels! I'm hungry!"

He had built a very violent army, which worked great for raiding, but there was no loyalty. These men were savages, which is why he had to prove he was the biggest savage of them all. Show no fear. Show no mercy. That had been what had kept him alive this long.

Connor went inside and jogged down the spiral staircase. The ground floor was dark. There were wooden shutters over all the windows, blocking out all natural light. He grabbed his guns and stepped outside.

His men were waiting for him.

"Today, we find the women who killed our friends. We're headed back to that little shack."

"Why? We've already been there and searched. There's nothing there," someone grumbled.

Connor put on the meanest face he could pull together, "Because they will be back. Where else they gonna go? They were living out there for a while. That means there is some good hunting. We need to get us a couple deer. I don't know about you guys, but I want some meat!"

There was a large cheer from the crowd, restoring Connor's confidence that he had them for at least another day. Today had to be the day they found the women or food. If not, things were going to get ugly.

He had heard rumors of another small group around the area. They didn't trade with anyone and kept to themselves. That was the group to hit. If they didn't trade, it was because they had everything they needed. Connor was going to find them. His men would trust his leadership and they could ride out the winter without worrying about food.

Connor had gained his following with the promise of a place to live out their days in comfort. Currently, his only thought was finding food and shelter. As the number of men traveling with him grew, things had gotten out of control.

Somehow, the lie had grown and evolved and it was about to blow up in his face. He had no control over the men he claimed to rule. They plundered with wild abandon. Killing and destroying with no rhyme or reason. He had screwed up. He should have reined them in. Saving and rationing the food supplies would have given him more power.

His only hope was to find this reclusive prepper group. He knew they would have what he promised his men. Once they found the group, he would establish his role as the leader. None of the men would ever question him again and his role as commander would be solidified. Connor knew if he could prove he knew what he was doing, he would never have to lift another finger again. His minions would do all the heavy lifting. He would be a king.

He had to find that group. He had no doubt in his mind they were close. They couldn't hide forever.

Chapter Nine

That night at dinner, there was little conversation—everyone was exhausted after their busy day shoring up defenses and working on the camo nets. Between playing with the goats and running around collecting material for the nets, Caitlin and Ryland could barely keep their eyes open during dinner and even volunteered to go to bed with very little encouragement from their parents. Chase had been impressed with the nets and promised to get them started on attaching the foliage they'd collected in the morning.

"I can go back to my house and grab more traps," Brenda said, out of the blue.

They had all retired upstairs and were just enjoying the peace and quiet.

"That's too dangerous," Chase said.

"I will be fine. We need more. The ten we have aren't enough. I had more in the barn, assuming they didn't take them."

No one had to ask. She was referring to McDaniels and his men.

"What if they're there waiting?" Willow asked her.

"I think after all this time, they've moved on."

"Megan and I will look," Wyatt said, nodding slowly. "We need to do more hunting. The meadow is close enough to your old place, we'll swing by."

"What? Are you sure your leg is healed enough to make the trek?" Megan asked.

"It's fine. Pretty much back to normal. We need more food. I checked the root cellar earlier. We can't risk going out in the winter if we don't have to. We may not even be able to walk if the snowfall is too high. We don't know how the snowshoes will hold up."

Megan knew he had a point. All of them were counting on hunting through the winter, but now they had another problem to consider besides the weather.

Going out hunting with McDaniels and his men actively looking for them was far too dangerous; especially since the Raiders had access to ATVs. There was no way they could outrun them if chased.

"He's right," Megan answered, turning to Brenda. "You'll be too easy to recognize and McDaniels has already met me. Just tell me where they are in the barn. You can stay here and keep working on the defenses. If Wyatt and I are already going to be out, it makes sense. We don't want to leave this place more vulnerable than it already is."

What Megan didn't say was that the more people roaming around the mountain, meant fewer people at the lodge to protect her daughter. Brenda was an excellent shot and she had already proven she would give her own life to protect Caitlin.

Brenda quickly explained where to find the traps in the back corner in an old box.

Wyatt stood, "We better get to bed. We'll be gone before the rest of you get up, so we'll see you by mid-afternoon."

Megan knew he was telling the group if they weren't home by then to come looking. He had already told them they would be around the meadow. That would give them a place to start their search. It was a good habit they had enforced since Megan and Caitlin had gotten lost in a storm.

With the threat of McDaniels, they had to be much more cautious. They couldn't go out scavenging or hunting without telling the others where they were headed.

Their lives depended on it.

Chase stood, "If I'm not up before you leave, can you wake me? I want to get some lists made so everyone knows what to do. I will be out on the property most of the day and won't be coming in."

Wyatt nodded, "Sure thing."

"Good night, everyone," Megan said, heading down the stairs.

She was thrilled to go hunting in the morning. Especially since that meant she and Wyatt got some time alone. He hadn't been able to do much the past few weeks and being alone in their room was not the same as being alone in the forest.

"I see that little skip," he said walking close behind her, putting his head into her neck. "You can't wait to get me alone, huh?"

She laughed, "You caught me. What more can a girl ask for, hunting with a big gun and spending time alone with her man."

"Actually, I was thinking we test out those bows and arrows we got."

Megan groaned. They had been target practicing, but it wasn't the same as aiming and pulling the trigger on a gun.

"How about you take a bow and I'll take my gun?"

He laughed, "Megan, you are going to run out of bullets eventually. You have to learn archery. It will ensure we have a way to put food on the table for the foreseeable future. You don't want us all to become vegetarians, do you?"

"Fine, we'll take the bow, but I'm taking my gun as well. We can't risk not bringing anything back. We'll try it your way and if it doesn't work, I'm shooting."

"Sounds like a plan. I'll grab the quiver and make sure we have plenty of arrows, just in case we lose any."

Megan was so amped for hunting, she hardly slept. It was still dark out, but she could hear the birds, which meant dawn would be breaking soon.

"Get up, sleepyhead, let's go hunting," she said, rousing the sleeping man next to her.

He didn't open his eyes as he replied, "You are way too giddy this early in the morning. I think there's something wrong with you."

She laughed, "I'm giddy because I'm imagining the big buck I'm going to bring home. Well, I'm going to shoot it and you are going to dress it and drag it back."

"I feel like you're only using me for my body," Wyatt said, opening one eye.

Megan gave his bicep a squeeze, "I am. Now, get up."

Wyatt was moving far too slow for her taste. She had been pacing, checking the bags and rechecking to make sure they had everything. She was carrying her hunting rifle. Wyatt would have the bow, along with his own rifle.

When he finally came out of the room, she saw he had his chest holster on as well with his .45 tucked neatly inside.

She walked over, stretched up on her tiptoes and gave him a

84

kiss. "Let's go."

"Did you get Chase up?"

"Yep. Let's go."

"Slave driver."

"You'll be thanking me when you sit down to eat a nice, juicy steak. If we don't hurry, the deer will already be down for their afternoon nap."

He rolled his eyes, "Yeah, yeah, I get it."

Megan and Wyatt both checked their gear one last time before putting on their headlamps. They didn't bother turning them on just yet. Saving battery power was important. They could navigate the area immediately outside the lodge in the dark. Once they made their way into the trees, Megan walked directly behind Wyatt. This allowed them to use only his light, conserving hers.

Placing her hand on his waist, she followed closely behind him as he made his way down the hill without using the well-worn trail or triggering a trap. Every once in a while, Megan would tighten her hand on him, but she managed to stay within his footsteps and they made their way without incident.

Breathing a sigh of relief, they made good time to the meadow, despite Wyatt slowing down on occasion to flex his ankle. Megan pestered him about doing too much too soon but he reminded her that all hands and feet were needed now.

They found somewhere to perch, while they waited for the deer to make their way into the meadow to graze. Wyatt gathered pine needles for them to sit on. There was a slight layer of frost when they first set out, but it was already melting away, leaving the ground nice and wet.

Megan enjoyed the comfortable silence between the two of them. She loved the fact they didn't have to talk to enjoy each other's company. They could simply be.

"There," he whispered, pointing to the edge of the meadow. "I see one coming in."

Megan peered through the scope on her rifle counting quietly.

"It's a ten-point!" she whispered with excitement.

Wyatt was nocking an arrow, preparing to take the shot.

Megan silently groaned. If he missed, the buck would be spooked and take off.

He looked at her, "I'm going to try. You can take the shot if I miss. You're good enough to hit a moving target, right?" Wyatt winked at her.

"You know I am."

She lined up the shot, keeping the buck in her focus. It had come through the trees and was casually walking towards them, stopping on occasion to take a bite of the wet grass.

Megan was coaching Wyatt. If he took the shot too soon, he would definitely miss. He had honed his archery skill to the point he could hit a target at about forty yards provided the target wasn't moving. She needed the buck far enough into the clearing that she would have the chance to take a shot before he made it to the trees. If the buck got too close to them, it would sense they were there and bolt. It was a fine line between too close and too far to hit.

When the buck was about forty-five yards away from them, she put her hand on the trigger. She would have seconds to shoot if Wyatt missed.

"Now," she said, barely audible.

Wyatt exhaled and released the bow string. The arrow whizzed through the quiet morning air sounding much louder than it probably was in reality. Picking its head up, the buck heard the sound and bolted as the arrow slammed into a tree behind where the buck had just stood.

Megan stayed calm, waited for the right moment and pulled the trigger. The buck dropped.

"Damn! That was an excellent shot!"

She stood, dusting off her backside, "I know. Let's go get our dinner."

It took them about an hour to field dress the buck. She

reminded Wyatt of the importance of dressing the deer right away. The body heat of the deer would spoil the meat quickly, which was why hunting season was during colder weather. It gave hunters wiggle room to get their harvest back and hung. Megan used her hunting knife to make a small incision in the belly and slicing upwards to the neck exposed the muscles. She then used the blade to puncture the muscles before turning the knife to use the gut hook and followed the same incision back down. Once the rib cage was exposed, she sawed through the bone to reveal the lungs and heart.

"You get to do the icky part," she told Wyatt.

He reached in and pulled out the intestines and internal organs, leaving it in one big pile in the meadow. Predators would be dining well tonight.

Once the deer had been dressed out, they loaded it into one of the game bags. Without a way to get the large animal back to the lodge without dragging it, she wanted to keep the meat as clean as possible. She unrolled the plastic game sled and between the two of them, they managed to get the deer onto it.

Wyatt pulled the sled while Megan kept her rifle at the ready as they walked to Brenda's house. They knew the Raiders were actively searching for Megan and Brenda.

Megan heard a noise. The look on Wyatt's face said he heard it too.

He dropped the sled rope and pulled his pistol from the holster.

Wyatt put his finger to his lips. She nodded. Her heart raced. They couldn't tell where the noise was coming from. She didn't know where to hide. They could be surrounded.

"There," Wyatt whispered pointing ahead and to the right.

Megan inched forward, her rifle trained in the direction. Wyatt walked beside her. They were prepared to shoot whatever came out of the trees.

A rabbit came barreling out from the woods hopping for the meadow.

Megan and Wyatt both laughed in relief.

When they got there, being careful to avoid the traps Brenda had told them about, Megan gasped when she saw what was left of Brenda's little house. The windows were smashed. Brenda's clothes had been strewn about and discarded.

"We need to go," Wyatt said, hyper alert now.

"I'll grab the traps," Megan said, running for the barn. There were too many to fit into her pack. She fit as many as she could and hung a few off the carabiner clips attached to her backpack. She put the rest on the sled with the deer.

Megan ended up helping Wyatt drag the large buck to cover more ground faster. They were in a hurry. Being outside the safety of the lodge made them nervous.

When they got close, Albert shouted to Chase they were back.

Chase came out to meet them and took over the dragging duties being careful not to get too close to any of the traps.

Megan looked at Wyatt. Sweat had broken out across his brow and he was favoring his bad leg.

"You good? Maybe take it easy the rest of the day?"

"I'm fine. It's just a little weak. If I don't work it, it only gets weaker."

She nodded, not wanting to push the issue. Rosie would say otherwise.

"This is great, Megan," Chase said with a huge smile on his face.

"How do you know I didn't get it?" Wyatt asked.

Chase laughed. "Am I wrong?"

"Well, the next one I guarantee will be one I got.

"Sure, buddy. Keep telling yourself that."

Megan didn't want to insult Wyatt, but he was not the best hunter. It was a timing thing. He was too used to hitting human targets that didn't have the instincts of a wild animal, instincts evolved over thousands of years.

"He did try that bow, though. You gotta give him credit for that," Megan added.

"I think we all better get used to that bow. Once we get all this other stuff taken care of, we will need to do a lot more practice," Chase said. "It seems like we are always behind the eight ball. No matter what we do or accomplish, there is always so much more to do."

All three nodded in agreement. No one said it, but they were all thinking the same thing; if there were more people in the group, they could divide and conquer. Many hands make light work. They would get more done and not have to worry about being unprepared or vulnerable.

Megan hated the thought, but Jack was right. If they had Evan's people here, the defenses would already be set up. Willow and Rosie would have help to get the camouflage net completed and there would be time to hunt and gather.

As it was, they were all working from sunup to sundown and beyond. They were exhausted and all of them could use a little downtime.

The ten minutes they got here and there to play catch with the kids was nice, but she wanted more. She wanted to spend more time with Caitlin just having fun. More people would mean less work and more time with Caitlin and Wyatt. But could she trust the newcomers?

Chapter Ten

Wyatt was not about to admit to anyone how bad his leg was killing him. He was very happy the deer hanger was only enough to support one animal at a time. That gave him about three days to rest before they went hunting again.

In the meantime, he was going to stay close to the lodge and rest when no one was looking.

His plan was soon completely tossed out the window though. Chase was waiting for him when he walked out of his bedroom, with the glint of a plan in his eye. Wyatt had thought everyone had already gotten started for the day.

"You good?"

Wyatt pulled his shoulders back, threw his chest out, "Of course. Why? What's up?"

Chase looked him up and down, focusing on Wyatt's limp.

"I'm fine. What do we need to do?" Wyatt asked, narrowing his gaze at Chase.

"I want to work on reinforcing the lodge. If they get through the traps out there, we need to be ready in here. If they breach the doors, I think you and I both know our chances of getting out of it alive are slim to none."

Chase would never talk like that in front of the women or kids, but given their history together in the military and Wyatt's time working in SWAT, he knew Wyatt would know exactly what he was talking about.

Wyatt huffed out a breath knowing it was time to get to work. He was all business now. The leg could rest tonight. There was no way he was going to let anything happen to his family. Not again.

Wyatt shook his head, "We can't let them get in."

"I agree, but we have to be ready for anything."

"Our main problem is that front door," Chase said pointing at the door they rarely used.

"Let's barricade it."

Chase whistled, "I don't know, man. That only gives us one way out. I don't like that at all."

Wyatt winked at him, "We can make another way out. My dad originally planned for that outdoor storage room to be a panic room."

"Is there access from the inside?" Chase asked.

Wyatt could see the excitement in his eyes.

"Well, not technically, but we could make one. That wall over there goes into the storage room. It wouldn't take much to remove the sheetrock. It is basically a hollow wall. We only need a big enough space for us to squeeze through. We wouldn't even have to take out any of the studs."

Chase slapped him on the back, "You are a frickin' genius." Chase paused, rubbing the side of his face with his thumb, "Or your dad was. Either way, it's perfect."

"We will need something to hide the hole in the wall."

Both men looked around the room, searching for an appropriate object.

Rosie shouted down from upstairs, "If you boys are going to be making a mess in my dining room, you'll be the ones cleaning it up."

Wyatt laughed, "It will actually be the kitchen, mom."

"Wyatt Morris, don't you dare destroy my kitchen!"

Chase held back a laugh.

Wyatt rolled his eyes. Big mistake.

"I know you just rolled your eyes, mister, and I am being completely serious. You better think long and hard about what you are going to do before you start tearing into walls."

"I will, mom."

He turned to Chase, "Let's go to the storage room and measure just how deep it goes in. That way we can get a better idea where to start tearing walls down."

He said the last few words nice and loud so his mom would hear.

She snorted in response. He could hear her complaining to Willow about the destruction of her kitchen.

Wyatt opened the side of the lodge that led to the hidden storage room. Chase walked behind him, stretching out a tape measure. They spent a few minutes, tapping walls and measuring distances. They were going to have to move a couple of the water barrels, but their plan would work. It was an excellent idea and one they wished they would have thought of earlier.

"Okay, so, we need to work on this and how do you want to take care of that front door?"

Wyatt winked, "Have no fear, my friend. I have a plan."

They walked towards the shed. They had been collecting building materials for months and with what his dad had left over from the construction of the lodge, they had quite a pile. Wyatt pointed to a portion of chain link fence that was on top of a pile of wood.

"That."

The fence was picked up with the intention of using it to build of an animal pen. It was a small section, maybe four feet wide and six feet high, but in this world, they knew everything could be useful.

Chase didn't look convinced, so Wyatt explained his plan.

"We nail that to the outside of the door. Think of it as bars on a door, but chain link instead. They aren't going to get through the fencing. Hopefully they won't even try," Wyatt explained. "Plus, we can still open the door for some fresh air."

Chase nodded, "Yeah, I guess that would work. Couldn't they just pry the nails out? A drill sure would be nice right about now."

"We have the old hand-crank drill, but we also have plenty of nails. I like the idea of shooting at non-moving targets while they pry the nails out," Wyatt said with a laugh.

Chase agreed and put it on their list of things to-do.

"We can also put up the barricades like Megan said Brenda had done. It's old-fashioned, but effective," Wyatt added.

"What about the windows," he said, looking up at the huge picture windows that overlooked the area. The windows were completely uncovered and allowed plenty of natural light into the lodge, but they were a vulnerability.

Wyatt shrugged, "There's nothing we can do about them. We'll hang the camo nets down, but other than that, we can't do much else. The only way someone is getting through those windows is with a ladder. They can break the windows, but they aren't coming in."

Chase had complained about the windows in the past. From a

security standpoint, they were a nightmare, but they were also necessary for group morale. If they didn't have plenty of natural light and the appearance of a wide-open space, the lodge would feel like a prison. It was a well-known fact people needed daylight and sunshine. Moods would suffer if they were cooped up in a dark space, day in and day out.

Both men walked around the lodge, paying careful attention to every detail.

"We need to cover the smaller windows on the ground floor. Obviously, nobody is coming through them, but we don't want them tossing anything in either," Chase said pointing to the one window in the kitchen that was still intact.

The other window had been boarded up after the storm sent a tree limb through it.

Wyatt walked back to the front of the lodge, looking up at the windows and imagining what it looked like inside.

"Do you think we can cut holes into the wood up there?" Wyatt asked Chase who was walking towards him. "You know like we had in our bunkers?"

Chase nodded, "You are just full of ideas today, aren't you? That would be helpful, but I don't know how thick that wood is. Maybe use a chisel and hammer?"

"We'll figure something out. Then we can have Megan and

Willow upstairs with guns. Megan has proven her skills time and again. With a bird's eye view up there, she can take out anyone that gets close. That will also keep them relatively safe."

"Okay, well, we have a lot to get done. You sure you're up to it?"

"I told you I'm fine. I was just a little stiff after being in bed. Once I get moving, I'll be just fine."

Chase didn't say it, but he clearly didn't believe him.

"Let's get to it," Wyatt said, walking away, gritting his teeth through the pain.

He wanted to drive home the point he was fine. He was back to his old self and ready, willing and able to fight. The leg would heal, eventually. He could get through the pain until it did. If a bit of pain now was the difference between beating McDaniels and being overrun by his raiders, he was willing to suffer. He hoped it was enough.

Chapter Eleven

Megan finished filling the water bucket for the goats—again. She had to take some extra time to hammer a few pieces of wood together to create a frame for the bucket. The frame was nothing more than a couple of eight-inch pieces of wood nailed to the corner of the fence, about twelve inches off the ground. This created a V for the bucket to sit in so she could pull it out if needed, but the goats wouldn't be able to tip the bucket. They had already spilled it several times, making their pen a muddy mess and wasting precious water.

"There, now you kids quit knocking it over!" she scolded.

Duke barked as if to add his own two cents.

"That's right buddy. They are being naughty goats."

Duke barked again.

Caitlin and Ryland came out of the lodge looking as if the weight of the world was on their shoulders.

"What's up guys?"

"Grandma says we have to get all this stuff done before we can play with the ball," Ryland said revealing how upset he was.

Caitlin looked at Megan, "Do we have to, mom? We just wanted to play. This is going to take us forever."

Megan smiled. Everything was so dramatic at this age. Even an apocalypse wasn't enough to rid the world of preteen attitude.

"Well, you guys are both old enough to help out. We have a lot to get done around here. Just think about how much fun you'll have when you're finished," she told them, smoothing back Caitlin's hair.

Ryland kicked at an invisible something on the ground, "Well, we better get started, Caity, or we'll never finish."

"How about this?" Megan started, doing her best to sound positive and upbeat. "You guys take care of your chores, Wyatt and I will take care of our chores, and if we all get done, we can play a game of baseball. Maybe we can talk everyone else into playing as well."

A huge grin spread across Caitlin's face, "Yes! I want to play baseball, mom!"

Ryland played it off, but she could tell he was excited by the idea.

"Okay," he said, "But this is a big list. I don't know if we can finish all of it."

"Then we'll have to wait until tomorrow or the next day. We can't play until the list is completed."

She hoped that would be enough incentive for them. They did tend to get a little off-task when they were together. Willow had decided to keep them separated when it came time for their school sessions. They would either laugh over the silliest things and lose focus or grumble at each other about every little thing.

They were best friends, which made all the adults happy. They kept each other occupied and the friendship provided a sense of normalcy.

Megan told them to stay close and headed towards the back door.

She could hear Ryland grumbling about how much they had to do. They were kids and shouldn't have to do so much work, but this was the new world they lived in.

Rosie was in the kitchen, cleaning up after breakfast.

"I saw the kids," Megan said.

Rosie started to laugh, "I know, you would think I sent them to dig their own graves." She held up the baseball. "Who knew this thing would wield so much power."

Megan laughed, "In the old days, we could threaten to take away the smartphones or television. Today, we get to take away their ball. Boy have things changed!"

"Yes, they have. They only have a few things to do. I asked them to collect more moss, some grass and twigs that are already on the ground. We are hoping to finish those nets today so Chase and Jack can get them hung."

"I can help. We aren't going hunting until the other deer is off the hanger."

Rosie grimaced, "Yes, that is why we need to finish the nets today so we can start processing that thing tomorrow. Don't get me wrong, I am excited for the meat, but I do not relish the slicing and dicing part of it."

Megan agreed with her. The luxury of going to a butcher for her meat was something she vowed never to take for granted again. That is, if the luxury was ever available again.

Jack came in through the back door. He didn't look happy.

"What's up?" Megan asked.

"Albert needs a break. He has been up in the lookout since daybreak. I have to go up, but I wanted to grab a jacket. It's chilly out there when you aren't working up a sweat."

Megan thought about it for a second, "I'll take the watch. That way you can keep working on the perimeter."

When it looked as if he was going to argue, she shook her head, "Don't even try to say something along the lines of me being a girl and all that. You all know I can shoot better than most of you and my eyes work just fine. I can also scream like a banshee if I need to. Just go back to what you were doing and I will relieve Albert."

Jack hesitated and looked towards Rosie.

"She'll be fine, Jack. Get some water before you head back out," his mother lectured.

"Okay, I'll grab my coat and then head out there. Thanks, Megan."

Megan quickly dressed, grabbed her rifle, threw some ammo in the coat pocket and walked to where Albert was waiting.

He crawled down the tree using the pegs that had been hammered in to make the climbing into the bird's nest easier and faster.

"This isn't going to work," he grumbled.

"What isn't?" Megan asked.

"I can't be the only person watching. We built two more bird's nests, but what's the point if only one of us is on watch at a time?"

He was right, but bringing in more people would mean having to trust more people. Megan just wasn't sure she was ready for that yet—she'd only just gotten used to trusting the lodge family.

"I know, Albert. Right now, everyone is busy trying to get the place fortified. Then we need to get food for the winter. There's so much to do. We are all taxed."

"Well, what good is it gonna do to have food if it's just going to get taken when those guys come looking?"

Albert stomped off without giving her the chance to answer.

Megan climbed into the bird's nest and took a few minutes to appreciate the view. No wonder Albert willingly spent so much time up here. It was gorgeous and so peaceful. In the distance, a mountain peak stood sentry. There was already bit of white at the top. Locals would call it the snowcap. It heralded winter was coming. When the cap melted away, it was officially spring by mountain standards. Her gaze moved downwards. She could see the stream gurgling below. Lush vegetation grew along each side. It looked like the type of picture she would have paid money for in the past.

It all looked so serene, but she knew that every few feet there was a deadly trap set. Their once peaceful property was now full of booby traps. The threat of someone trying to take it all away was very real. It ruined the splendor and the beauty of the magnificent view.

Megan got comfortable. Albert had a small, folding fishing chair he had carried up making it easy for him to maintain a lookout and rest his knee at the same time.

The more she looked around, the more she realized this one viewpoint wasn't enough. They needed more eyes. She would like to have a lookout at night, but it didn't make a lot of sense. It would be next to impossible to see. However, they could have someone near the lodge on watch. That way if those men happened to get through all the traps, they would have a chance to fight back.

Megan spent about an hour in the bird's nest before Albert hollered at her he was back. She had been enjoying herself. It was so peaceful and gave her plenty of time to think.

She and Wyatt were going hunting again tomorrow. She needed to talk to him about their future here at the lodge. Things had to change.

Chapter Twelve

"I don't like it," she said, trying to get comfortable on her perch of pine needles overlooking the meadow where they had scored the last deer.

Megan knew she sounded like a petulant child, but it was the truth.

"Megan, we have to think long term. We need to be realistic. We've been living in a bubble and it's about to burst in a big, terrible way," Wyatt reasoned.

She refused to look at him and kept staring out into the meadow. Their hunting trip wasn't quite as nice and enjoyable as the last time.

He had started in about inviting Evan's group to the lodge last night in bed and hadn't let up.

"Wyatt, we don't know those people. I mean, Bryan and Evan, sure. They seem decent enough. Amy, Sandra and Tara, I think they're okay, but that is a handful compared to the twenty or so you are talking about bringing in."

"They bring in people all the time and they've been just fine."

She spun around and glared at him.

"Yeah, that has worked out real well for them, hasn't it?"

He rolled his eyes, "The newcomers aren't killing them. McDaniels is harassing them because they're easy targets. We aren't exactly a force to be reckoned with. Should I send my mom out with a rolling pin and tell them to shoo when they come knocking on the door?"

She groaned in frustration.

"I know. I know we need more people. I just wish there was another way. I wish we had more time to get to know them. Seriously, I wish we could run background checks on each one of them, you know?"

He laughed, "Oh, the good old days when you could stalk someone before you actually had to talk to them."

"I get that more people presents a stronger force. It means more people shooting at the bad guys, but it also means we have to trust more people. The odds that there is a bad apple in the group are high. We can't expect to meet twenty strangers and they'll all be good, honest people who won't stab us in the back or cause problems."

It was Wyatt's turn to groan in frustration.

"You are only as strong as your team. You have to trust the guy standing next to you, fighting against a common enemy," he said more to himself than to Megan.

She knew he was thinking back to his days in the Navy as a

SEAL. Combat required him to trust his friends that were standing beside him with his life.

"What about food, beds, water and all that stuff?" Megan asked.

"If they're here, they hunt and work. Yes, it will tax our resources, but the more people out hunting, planting and collecting edible plants, the more food coming in. It isn't like we are going to invite them in so they can have a vacation and sit around. Everyone will be working together."

"Shh!"

Wyatt watched as Megan held up her rifle and carefully moved the barrel just a hair to the right. She could feel his eyes on her, but she didn't let that interrupt her focus on the doe standing in the meadow. Megan watched as the deer meandered into the meadow, stopping to nibble on grass and bushes. The deer froze and stood stock still, looking up into the trees surrounding the meadow. Megan could tell by her stance that she was going to bolt at any second. She pulled the trigger and watched the doe drop where she stood.

She turned to look at Wyatt to gloat. But the look on his face stopped her from doing so. He was looking at her with such pride and love it made her heart swell.

"You got her, baby, you got her!"

Megan grinned, "Yep, now guess what you get to do?"

"I hate that you only use me for the dirty work. I'm so much more than that!"

"Come on, Wyatt, you know you enjoy getting a little…dirty," Megan teased.

"Only with you, baby."

They both laughed as they made their way down the hill to take care of the doe as they talked about the fresh steak they hoped to eat tonight.

Megan knew they had come to an understanding about Evan's group. Wyatt wanted to take it slow, but they were going to improve the relationship. They needed to be stronger allies and that meant talking more often than once a month.

Deep down, Megan knew it was for the best, but it still made her nervous. It would start along a path that would force her to let more and more people into her circle of trust. She would just have to keep her guard up and pay attention. It would be a tense few months, but she would do whatever it took to keep her family safe. If Wyatt thought this was the way to go, so be it. She trusted him implicitly. He would never do anything to put any of them in jeopardy.

Time would tell if it was the right choice.

Between the two of them, they dragged the doe back to the

lodge. It was a repeat of the other day, but a tad easier due to the doe being so much smaller. There was a lot of celebrating and everyone praised Megan for her killer hunting skills when they returned to the lodge.

She felt a great deal of pride at being such an intricate part of the group. She looked around for Wyatt and saw him and Albert in the corner, quietly talking. She had a feeling she knew what he was doing.

She casually walked to where the two men were huddled together.

"Can you get Greg on the radio?" Wyatt asked.

Albert shrugged, "I could try, but he doesn't always answer. I haven't heard from him in a couple of days."

"Do you normally hear from him more often than that?" Wyatt asked.

"Eh, usually it's once a day. Just a quick hello and check to see how things are going."

Megan was impressed Albert had made a friend. The two had never actually met, but they seemed to have a lot in common.

Wyatt looked concerned. Megan suspected he was worried McDaniels had gone back and either killed them all or maybe took the radio.

"I'll give it a try. Maybe the solar panel wasn't working right. Or maybe the old codger couldn't figure out how to plug it in," Albert joked.

Megan could see the worry on his face as well. He was concerned for his friend, but was doing his best to play it off.

"How about you do that after we have some dinner. Better chance he will be settled in for the night and around to hear your call. Right?" Megan asked, patting Albert on the shoulder and steering him towards the kitchen.

"Yeah, you're right. He can't sit by that stupid radio all day."

They all pitched in to help cut the meat into steaks. They got busy cutting the rest into strips to dry near the fire.

Megan hoped with the addition of the doe, plus the other deer they'd already prepped, they would have enough food to get through winter. It would be tight, but they could do it.

If the other group came to the lodge, there was no way they could feed that many people for three months.

She wasn't going to hope for the best when it came to their food supply. If the other group was coming, she was going to do everything she could to pad their food stores. The risk of running out of food terrified her almost as much as McDaniels and his gang. She couldn't imagine not being able to feed her child.

Chapter Thirteen

Megan heard the shout before she saw Jack race through the trees that surrounded the outer perimeter of the lodge and towards her. Something was drastically wrong.

Her heart was pounding so hard she thought for sure it would bounce right out of her chest.

She didn't know whether to run towards him to offer help or run inside and lock the lodge down.

Caitlin!

"Caitlin! Ryland! Get inside! Get in the lodge now!" she screamed not willing to take any chances.

The kids didn't ask twice, dropping the game of ball they were playing and ran for the back door. Willow and Rosie heard her shout and popped their heads out of the mudroom door. Megan waved them back in. She needed them to keep the kids safe.

"What is it?" she asked Jack who was breathing hard.

"They're here!"

Megan felt like everything came to a stop. Her legs felt like lead. She couldn't move. She couldn't speak. She just stared.

This was what they had been expecting and preparing for, but they weren't ready. Not even close.

"Wyatt?" she managed to squeak out.

"Fine, he is talking with them now."

Megan couldn't believe what she heard. What?

"Talking to them? What? Are you kidding me? What does he hope to accomplish? Why did you leave him, Jack?"

Jack's brow furrowed in frustration, "He told me to come back and let you know."

"Me? Why me? What does he want me to do?"

Jack was getting irritated, "Go out and talk to them, Megan. Chase is with him. Brenda and Albert are each in a bird's nest, keeping watch, just in case."

Megan considered shaking Jack, but didn't think it would help. The man was rattled and wasn't making any sense at all.

"Jack," she said slowly and with the voice she used when she talked to Caitlin when she was having a nightmare. "Jack, I need you to take a deep breath and start from the beginning."

He glared, put his hands on his hips and looked her straight in the eye, "Get your butt out to the stream. Wyatt is there waiting with Evan's group. Brenda and Albert are each in a bird's nest keeping a lookout."

When she looked at him with confusion, it was his turn to use slow and careful words.

"Go. Out. There. Now."

"I'm not an idiot, Jack, but you said they. Who is 'they'? I thought you meant McDaniels." She groaned. "Never mind. I'm going."

She started to walk away. Jack called her name. She stopped and turned back, "Be smart. Do what you think is right. I trust you."

She smiled and nodded, "Thank you, Jack. I will. Take care of the kids."

Megan sprinted out to the stream. When she saw Wyatt and Chase on the ground next to an older man, she gasped. Each of the people standing there, looking lost and forlorn, had blood on them. She couldn't tell if it was their own blood or blood from their family and friends.

She rushed through the stream, not caring that her feet got wet.

"What happened?" she asked, dropping next to Wyatt to offer assistance. She recognized the man whose leg had been sliced open. She couldn't remember his name.

Wyatt handed her a strip of cloth and she quickly tied it around the wound.

"Tighter," he ordered, spurring Megan to do as he asked.

"We need to stop the bleeding," he explained. "Make it good

and tight so we can get him back to the lodge."

Wyatt turned his head and yelled to the sky, "Brenda! We are gonna need you down here for this."

Brenda responded that she was on her way.

They waited and watched a few seconds before Wyatt declared he was ready to move him.

"Hang tight for a second," he told Chase before pulling Megan away from the crowd.

"What happened?" she asked again.

"McDaniels. He raided them and this time, he didn't go easy. He killed a lot of them. This is all they have left." He looked away before adding, "They found the big cabin."

Megan groaned. She knew what that meant. They would have been completely wiped out of supplies. Megan looked back at the group to do a head count. There were ten that she could see. She quickly looked for little Amy and sighed with relief when she spotted her clinging to her mother. Evan was standing close to them, as if to shield them from anything else that may come their way.

"What do we do?" she whispered.

Wyatt gently grabbed her chin and forced her to look at him, "It's up to you. We've all made up our minds. What do you want to do here, Megan?"

"Me? You can't put that on me!"

His eyes said it all. It was on her. She was the one who had been arguing against the group joining theirs. She was the one concerned for her daughter's safety. They were willing to turn these people away if she said no.

Megan looked at Wyatt and knew what he wanted her to say. He was the kind of guy that was a natural hero. He saved people. So did Jack and Chase. Rosie would open her door to anyone. Albert, despite his grumblings, would probably do the same. Brenda didn't really have a say yet, but Megan had a feeling she would side with the rest of the group.

A million thoughts flashed through her mind. Food. Water. Caitlin.

She looked back at the newcomers and saw Tara's blank stare. One arm was gripped tightly around her daughter and the other around Evan's waist. Evan was supporting her and she was supporting Amy.

Megan could easily identify with Tara. That could be her and Wyatt with Caitlin. Would she expect someone to help them and take them in should the lodge be attacked and their family members violently murdered?

Megan looked back at Wyatt, "Okay."

He leaned forward, kissed her on the forehead and whispered, "Thank you."

"Let's go invite our new members in," she said, holding his hand and walking towards the group. Bryan and Greg were supporting the injured man between them. Evan looked at Wyatt and he gave a quick nod, which prompted Evan into action. He picked up Amy and told her to hold on tight.

"We can walk downstream a little and use the crossing there," Wyatt told them.

Evan's people didn't seem to hear him. They kept walking and went right through the stream.

Megan figured they were tired, hungry and ready to find shelter. They had all been through a horrendous ordeal and were in shock. Bryan forced a smile at Megan as he walked by, supporting his friend.

Wyatt waited until everyone was across.

"Stay vigilant," he said in a loud voice aimed upwards.

"Will do. Those people are savages. I will personally take it upon myself to shoot as many as I can," Albert said from up above.

Brenda had come down from her perch to inspect the injured man.

"I'll need to clean and stitch that up. Who's taking my place up there?" she gestured towards the bird's nest she had just vacated.

Wyatt looked around, "Chase, can you take over watch while Brenda patches this guy up?"

Chase nodded and quickly took over the other watch station. They had to be more vigilant than ever now.

Chapter Fourteen

The arrival of the group at the lodge was chaotic. Rosie went into drill sergeant mode, directing people where to go and who to help. She had the injured man laid on the dining table where Brenda was tending to his wounds.

Megan stayed out of the way, but kept a close watch on everything that was happening. Brenda was calm, cool and collected. Her training and experience on the battlefield had kicked in.

There were people crying quietly and others walking about the lodge, checking things out. Her anxiety was increasing with every whisper, command or look in her direction.

Wyatt was coming down the stairs and spotted her standing in the corner. He walked towards her, grabbed her by the hand and took her into their room.

"You okay?" he asked her with genuine concern.

"Yeah, it just… makes me nervous. There are a lot of people here and there is no way we can watch all of them, every minute."

"I don't think we need to watch them all, every minute. Megan, they've just been through something horrible. They need us. I don't think they have the energy or courage to try to hurt us or take this place from us."

119

She felt like a jerk. She was being selfish. They had been alone for so long, it felt strange to have so many people invade her small, safe world.

"It's fine. I mean, I know. I just, well, it's just a lot. I'll be fine," she said, giving a small, tight-lipped nod of her head. "I just need some time to get used to everything. It's so much."

He grinned, "Yeah, there does seem to be a lot happening. I'm sure things will settle down by this evening. We just need to figure out where to go from here."

Wyatt turned to leave. She grabbed his arm, "What happened to them?"

"I don't know the details. There wasn't time to get into it, but I am going to find Bryan or Evan or both and find out what the hell happened out there."

"I'm coming with you," she said, grabbing a sweater out of the closet. The air outside was chilly and there was no way they could have a private conversation in the lodge. The last thing she wanted to do was expose any of the kids to the horrors of what had happened back at Evan's camp. It was obvious it wasn't meant for kids' ears.

Wyatt and Megan walked out the back door. With the front door barricaded, it was their only option. Megan wasn't sure it was the best idea, but Jack and Wyatt assured her it was as safe as could be.

Evan and Bryan were busy putting up the old Army tent that had been stashed away in the storage shed. Megan's nose instantly crinkled as she thought about how stinky it must be. The tent was huge and would be big enough for all ten people in their group. But with the chill of winter approaching, how long they could stay in the tent was questionable.

She watched the two men working in silence. They both appeared to be lost in thought. As they approached, she noticed blood on Evan's sleeve. Bryan had speckles of blood all down the side of his jeans.

She shuddered. They had been through something horrendous. They were wearing the blood of their friends and people they loved. Both men were so focused on protecting and caring for the remaining people in their group, they hadn't even taken the time to clean up. She had a whole new respect for them both.

"Hey," Wyatt said as they approached.

Evan and Bryan both jumped turning quickly, eyes wide and fists bunched. Wyatt had startled them.

"Hey. What's up?" Bryan asked, his body language relaxing as they approached.

He was holding a couple of tent poles, trying to get them to fit together. His hands were clumsy and shaking. She reached out and helped him slide the two poles together. His eyes met hers and just stared. Megan wanted to hug him and promise him it would all be okay, but didn't figure that was what he needed in this moment.

"What happened out there?" Wyatt asked.

"It was a surprise attack in the middle of the night," Bryan started. "There was no rhyme or reason to it."

"So, they found the big cabin?" Wyatt asked.

Evan sighed, dropped the poles he was working on and nodded.

"I guess we better explain why we just showed up at your door. Is there somewhere we can talk?"

Wyatt looked around. Jack was filling water jugs. A couple of Evan's men were leaning against the back wall of the lodge, talking in soft voices.

"How about the bench?" Megan suggested.

The foursome walked to the spot that Megan had grown so fond of. They had added a couple of chairs made from some old tires they had found down the hill.

They all sat down, with Wyatt and Megan sitting on the bench. Bryan and Evan sat across from them on the tire chairs. Bryan was looking at his hands and then his pants. He was staring at a large, dried spot of blood.

"What happened?" Wyatt repeated.

Evan met his eyes, "They slaughtered us. There is no other word for it. McDaniels has lost his mind. He is all that is evil. This time was completely different—once he found the larger cabin. He killed…children just because he could. He murdered the women trying to protect the children. Why? Why would he do that?"

Megan felt a thick knot tightening in her stomach and had the sudden urge to vomit. Wyatt reached out and put a hand on her knee to comfort her.

"I don't know. What provoked him? You said in the past he came and took what he wanted and then left."

Bryan, still staring at the blood, spoke up, "The men all seemed different. Like they were together, but not really in it together. One of the men was questioning McDaniels. He shot him. Another one of the men looked as if he was going to say something when McDaniels turned the gun on him. He didn't shoot him, though. He shot one of the young women who had just come to our camp a couple months ago."

"When they found the large cabin," Evan said quietly. "They took what they could carry and then burned it to the ground."

Megan gasped. "I'm so sorry. I don't even know what to say,

but I'm sorry."

Wyatt nodded in understanding.

"And that's why you're here."

Bryan nodded, "We have nothing left. No food, no shelter, nothing. We're on the brink of winter. We didn't want to come here, man. You have to know that. We know how difficult things are, but we didn't have a choice. We couldn't leave the rest of the group out there exposed to such evil."

"It's okay. I would have done the same thing," Wyatt assured him, reaching across to squeeze Bryan's shoulder. "We'll figure something out. Are you sure they didn't follow you?"

Bryan shook his head, "We had someone hang back to make sure. McDaniels and his men were completely loaded down with all our stuff. I'm positive they were headed back to their own camp."

Megan looked at the men she had come to know as strong and courageous. They looked defeated. Their shoulders were slumped forward and they both had a look in their eyes that said they were broken.

"We're going to kill them all," Megan stated, determined.

All three men looked at her. No one smiled or chided her for saying something so outrageous.

Wyatt's hand gripped her knee lightly. "Damn straight we are. That kind of evil needs to be eradicated. It will spread like cancer if we don't get rid of it."

"I hope so. Those people are savages," Bryan said through gritted teeth.

"We have some chores to get done if we are going to make all of this work," Wyatt said, standing up. "You guys want to take a few minutes and clean up? I can get Jack to help you with that tent. Then we will need to talk with Chase about how we are going to make sure this place is secure. With all of us here, it will be easier to rotate watch. We need to be on guard 24/7. I have a feeling McDaniels is going to find his way up here sooner rather than later."

Bryan extended his hand to Wyatt, "Thanks. I know this is a huge burden and I promise we will do everything we can to lighten the load. I can't tell you how much we appreciate this."

Evan nodded his head, "No matter what happens, please promise me you will take care of Tara and Amy. They have both been through so much. They don't deserve what has happened to them."

Megan blinked several times to clear the tears from her eyes. Evan was a good guy. She hadn't been convinced of that fact early on, but now she could see his love and devotion to the woman that fate had dropped on his doorstep.

Wyatt promised him they would be taken care of. They all walked back to the lodge with a newfound energy and strength. Things were about to become very dangerous, but Megan knew there would be strength in their numbers.

Chapter Fifteen

Willow and Rosie were busy rushing back and forth in the kitchen and Megan could see the stress etched in the lines on their faces. They weren't chatting or joking like they normally did. They were cooking for twenty instead of ten. That doe they had just butchered would be gone in no time. Their food supply was barely going to carry them through and now they had an extra ten mouths to feed.

Tara was peeling potatoes at the end of the breakfast bar with Amy by her side, chopping the potatoes into small chunks. The pile of potatoes waiting to be peeled was alarming. Megan could see the food supply dwindling right before her eyes.

They had to do something quick.

Megan had helped the men get the tent set up and was coming in to get blankets for them. They had thought they had plenty— they'd even considered trading the surplus—but with this many people, they were barely going to have enough. When Megan walked upstairs, she was surprised by the scene.

Sandra, Greg and a little boy she hadn't met yet were all sitting on the couch. It was very odd to see strangers in the lodge. It wasn't like they had company on a regular basis.

She quickly went to the closet and grabbed a couple of blankets. They didn't have pillows, but she doubted that would be a big problem.

She walked back downstairs, taking in the sounds of people talking. They were everywhere. Everywhere she looked there were people in small groups, huddled together.

"Megan, everyone will be sleeping inside, except for Evan and Bryan," Rosie told her as she crossed the kitchen.

"What?"

How in the world were they going to fit all those people in the lodge?

"It's too cold out, but Evan and Bryan insisted they would be fine. We will use the floor upstairs and down here around the fire."

Megan wanted to argue, but didn't. It wasn't her lodge—this was Rosie's. What she said, went.

"Okay, I'll just set these here," she said referring to the extra blankets, "and take a couple out to the tent."

Rosie smiled. It wasn't a real Rosie smile. The smile was polite and strained, much like a politician would paste on when meeting new constituents.

Megan was going to find Wyatt and have a talk with him. They needed to set some ground rules if this new situation was going to work. The amount of bodies in the lodge was sure to cause problems for everyone.

*   *   *

There was a rush of activity as Rosie and Willow dished up dinner for everyone. Unlike their normal practice of putting the dishes on the table and everyone helping themselves, they were now being served. It was a way to ration the food. Megan wasn't sure she was comfortable with it, but knew that was the way it had to be.

Wyatt had already promised her a group meeting after dinner to go over the concerns she had as well as the rest of the group. Apparently, she wasn't the only one who had been complaining to him.

All around the table, there were individual conversations about sleeping, food and taking turns using the outhouse. Wyatt was acting as a mediator, trying to answer as many questions and concerns as possible.

Megan silently watched from her seat in the corner. She had to put some space between her and the many bodies crowding around the table and breakfast bar.

"You ready?" Chase said standing up from his spot on the floor. He had given up his seat at the table so the women and children could sit down.

One of the men from Evan's group, Garrett, stood up and nodded. Megan could tell he wasn't thrilled about having watch duty. The kid was young, probably in his early twenties. He was tall and lanky and had that frat boy look about him. She was guessing he had been young and full of excitement about his future before the EMP struck. Now, he looked as if he carried the weight of the world on his shoulders.

It was dark and cold and sitting in the trees for hours would be miserable, but it had already been decided it was an absolute necessity. They couldn't take the chance of being caught off-guard now that McDaniels' Raiders were in the area. Wyatt had wanted Chase to stay for their impromptu meeting, but Chase wasn't about to leave the fate of the lodge in the hands of strangers.

It was decided an original member would always be on watch with a member from the new group. This made everyone feel a little better.

They had decided to meet in Wyatt and Megan's room. It was cramped, but they squeezed in.

"How's everyone doing?" Wyatt asked the original lodge members.

Rosie and Willow both looked at each other, but didn't say anything.

Albert surprised them all, "I'm glad for the extra hands. We need help getting this place secured. With more eyes to keep watch and more hands to get the heavy lifting done, we have better odds of beating this crazy dude at his own game."

Brenda nodded in agreement, "Wars are won by sheer force and strategy. Now we have both. We can win this war."

Megan knew the veterans would say something along those lines. Brenda was career military. Everything she did was programmed by her extensive training and experience in the Army.

"Can we trust them?" Megan had to ask.

Jack shrugged, "Little late for that."

Megan glared at him. He smiled in return.

"She's right," Wyatt spoke up. "I don't think we can trust them all just yet. There are a couple of guys I am not sure of. I think Bryan, Evan and Greg are solid. Sandra and Tara are harmless as well as that other little boy."

"We watch them. We keep certain things to ourselves for now, like the escape hatch," Jack said referring to the wall in the kitchen they had just finished opening up into the store room.

"What about the root cellar?" Willow asked. "We can't exactly hide that forever."

Everyone nodded in agreement, "They'll know it's there. All

we can do is keep an eye on things. Like Jack said, that ship has sailed. We're in it now. We do what we can to keep some things to ourselves, including the stashes that are buried around the property. If we want them to trust us, we can't be shady," Wyatt reasoned.

"Are we going to shadow them, like we did—" Megan stopped. She was going to say like they did with Brenda, but considering Brenda was in the room, it felt wrong.

"It's okay. I knew and I appreciated you being careful. It made me feel a little better knowing you didn't just let anyone into your group," Brenda assured her.

Jack spoke, "I don't think we need to shadow anyone. Well, maybe those two guys. One's name is Garrett; I don't remember the other one."

"David," Brenda stated.

"Okay, David and Garrett stay on our radar. We know the rest and I think we all feel pretty comfortable with them, right?"

"What about the guy Brenda fixed up?" Jack asked.

No one said anything.

"Did anyone talk with him?"

Silence.

Brenda spoke up, "His injury wasn't that bad. He'll be up and walking in a matter of days. Or he should be."

"Then we do what we can to feel them all out, while watching them," Wyatt said.

Everyone agreed.

"The kids need to be watched by one of us. I trust Tara and Sandra, but I would feel better if one of us was nearby," Willow added.

They all agreed and promised one of the adults in the room would always be near the kids.

"What about the guns?" Albert asked.

"I think for now, those are kept under wraps. We don't need to flaunt what we have. If we are under attack, we will distribute the guns, but for now, let's leave them out of sight," Wyatt offered.

Megan hesitated, but finally had to say what was on her mind, "I think one of us needs to be on watch here at the lodge all night. At least until things settle down a bit."

Everyone quickly agreed.

"Okay, anything else?" Wyatt asked. "If you have something on your mind, now is the time to say it."

He looked around the group. No one said anything.

"Alright, I think we have some ground rules and we will go from here. Tomorrow we are going to have to work out some plans for getting more food and stepping up our security even more. We will get the other group in on all of that. There is no reason for us to do all the work. With all of us working together, I think this could work," Wyatt said, sounding pleased with the outcome of the meeting.

Megan hoped his prediction proved to be true. As it was, she was feeling over crowded. Finding any privacy now was going to be very difficult. She took a moment to look around their little room. This would be her sanctuary to get away from the crowd.

It took an hour to get everyone settled into place. Garrett was going to sleep in the tent with Evan and Bryan. The man grumbled about it being cramped. Megan had to bite her tongue. Jack had placed a hand on her elbow to remind her of her manners.

Amy was sleeping with Caitlin. And the little boy, Frankie, was crashing on the floor next to Ryland. Rosie had insisted the injured man sleep downstairs instead of trying to climb the stairs. It was hectic, but once everyone settled down, Megan realized she kind of liked having a full lodge. It just felt stronger.

Chapter Sixteen

Connor McDaniels sat in front of the massive stone fireplace, deep in thought, as he stared at the dancing flames. The whiskey in his hand was going down smooth, settling his nerves. The leather chair cradled his weary body. If he wasn't so worried about one of his men slitting his throat while he slept, he would have dozed off right where he was sitting.

As it was, he couldn't—not if he wanted to see another day. Today's raid had been fruitful. They had scored a great deal of food and supplies. The men were in the large living room downstairs celebrating. They were drunk. Their hoots of laughter and the occasional shouts helped keep him awake.

He hoped the score would help settle things down in the group. The men were restless. They were on edge and losing confidence in his ability to be the leader he promised to be. He'd heard rumblings and knew mutiny wasn't far off if he didn't get control of things.

Shooting his man during the raid had driven home a point. He was the boss. He was not to be questioned. Connor surprised himself with his ability to be so ruthless. All those years of being rejected by society had cultivated the man he was today.

He didn't need to be accepted, but he did want to be feared. He couldn't afford anyone leaving. Every man who joined their forces made them stronger. Connor needed an army. That was the only way he could live. It wasn't like any of the little prepper groups they had encountered along the way would ever invite them in.

They were on their own. Together they could conquer the world, but divided they would surely all be killed. He prided himself on his ability to out think most people. These men were pawns and he manipulated them for his own gain. He would never be satisfied simply with surviving—he wanted to be set up.

When they'd found this house months ago tucked away in the woods, Connor knew he had struck gold. It resembled a castle with the stone walls and the large, heavy wooden doors. When he saw the house, he had decided it would be his.

He had walked right up to the front door and used the massive black iron door knocker. When the door opened, an older man was holding a sawed-off shotgun in his face. Connor remembered laughing at the man.

A quick shout was all it took for his own men to storm the house. The older couple inside hadn't stood a chance. When they gained entry to the stone fortress, they were richly rewarded. There was a cellar loaded with food, water and cases of liquor and beer. They had struck gold.

The couple were true preppers. Their home was built to withstand an attack, but with just the two of them to defend it, they were no match for Connor and his men.

Connor took the last drink of whiskey from his glass and stood. He wanted to check the cellar and see where they stood. When they had first come here, they hadn't thought much about the future or the winter. They had eaten until they were full every day and the food was being depleted at a rapid rate.

The recent raid would provide some cushion, but they needed more food if they were to maintain their current way of living throughout the winter. If the men thought he was failing in his duties to provide them with the cushy lifestyle they were enjoying, they would turn on him.

They would either leave or kill him. Connor couldn't let that happen. He was never one to give up. When he saw an opportunity, he took it. If he couldn't find one, he would make one. He was going to have to find that other group.

Chapter Seventeen

Wyatt had to count to ten and regain his composure before he lost his cool. The morning started off with a bang. There were people everywhere it seemed. It was chaotic, which just made everything stressful. No one had any real direction or purpose, which meant there were people in the way.

He had to get a hold on it and fast. He could see his mother getting frustrated with all the women trying to help her in the kitchen. There was no one leading the way. Nobody knew what to do, so everyone was trying to do everything—including the kids.

Megan was silently fuming in the corner. She had been trying to get in a word with Caitlin, but with all the commotion, it was next to impossible. The kids were feeding off the frenzy and going a little wild. There were at least five different conversations going on in various parts of the lodge. Everyone was trying to talk over each other.

Enough was enough. He walked back into the bedroom, grabbed a notebook off the dresser and headed into the fray.

He climbed onto one of the chairs at the table and whistled. It quieted the room somewhat, but not completely. He whistled again.

"Listen up," he said in a loud commanding voice.

The entire lodge fell silent. The small group upstairs slowly walked down and stood against the stairwell.

All eyes were on him.

"Listen, everyone. We need to get some jobs established. There is a lot that needs to be done. This is an all-hands-on-deck situation."

He turned to look at Caitlin and Amy who were giggling quietly on the floor, "Cait. Amy. That includes you girls. We need everyone's help. Evan. Bryan. Let's sit down and go over who does what best. Everyone else, please finish eating and get ready for a busy day."

He stepped off the chair and watched as everyone went in different directions. He hoped to God this would work.

Evan and Bryan pulled up chairs at the table.

"We need food. We need to build a new shelter and we need to work on upping our defenses. We also need to have at least two people on guard duty. Albert is out there with David now. Let's come up with a schedule so no one is out there for more than four hours at a time."

The men nodded in agreement.

"Okay," Wyatt started. "Who is great with a bow? I gotta say, the ammunition is dangerously low so we need to conserve what we have."

Bryan and Evan looked at each other, "Our best bow hunter was killed. Garrett isn't too bad, though."

Wyatt winced. He wasn't sure if he trusted Garrett yet. His hope was to send Megan out as well. He wasn't going to send Megan out with Garrett alone.

"Okay, we'll come back to that."

Jack came over to the table, pushing his hair out of his face.

"We need to build some kind of housing, like yesterday," he said. A long piece of hair flopped in his face again. He pushed it back, showing his frustration.

Evan smiled at him, "What you need to do is get a haircut unless you're going for some kind of Johnny Depp look, which I gotta say isn't working for you."

Jack rolled his eyes, "I happen to like my look and so does my wife." He leaned in and very quietly whispered, "She is the absolute worst when it comes to cutting hair. My mom, well if I want a bowl cut, she can hook me up."

All four men laughed. Wyatt had been trimming his own hair. He imagined he probably resembled a bit of a shaggy dog himself. In the grand scheme of things, a stylish do wasn't a big deal. Although it would be good to get a nice cut and feel like a normal man again.

Evan and Bryan exchanged a look. That is when Wyatt noticed

how normal their own hairstyles looked. Like they had just visited a salon. Not a barber with a pair of clippers, but an actual style.

"Why do you guys look like you just stepped off some photoshoot?" Wyatt asked. He was a little irritated. Their camp had been raided and they were starving, yet they both managed to keep their hair in perfect condition. Bryan smiled, "Our personal stylist insists we keep up with our appearance. I'm surprised she hasn't tackled you and went after that mess of hair on your head," he said to Wyatt.

"Who?" Jack asked all business.

"Tara. She was some big-time hair stylist before all this went down. At first we thought it was silly, but it helps her and it does make us feel a lot better. You need to have some of those little things to help keep you sane," Bryan explained.

Wyatt thought about it for a second and could see the reasoning behind it; anything that makes you feel more human is valuable.

"We'll talk to her. Schedule everyone for a haircut sometime over the next few days. The first cut takes a little longer. She says she has to see what works. Once she gets the style down, it's a quick upkeep every couple of weeks. Like Bryan said, she loves to do it. Says it reminds her of the good old days," Evan added.

Wyatt jotted down Tara's name and wrote hair beside it.

"Okay, now that we have the most important business out of the way, let's move onto less important matters like, oh, food," he said.

"David is a killer mechanic. He was working on a generator for the large cabin before everything went south. You have a generator?"

Wyatt nodded, "Yes, but what's the point if there is no fuel?"

"He was working on creating a hydroelectric setup. Water would run downhill, turning a wheel and it produced electricity. I really don't know the ins and outs, but he had it all figured out," Bryan explained.

Wyatt jotted the information down. He didn't see the importance of that skill right then, but this spring, it would be great to get electricity going.

"How about we put David with Jack on the new lodging. Evan, are you up for that as well?"

Evan nodded, "Yep, count me in."

"I'll go hunting with Megan and Garrett. If we can take two deer, that will give us a good start on our food supply. We'll need all three of us to get them back here. Jack, do you think you can throw up another deer hang?"

Jack nodded, "Yeah, I'll have Ryland and Frankie help me with that."

"Okay, we will have the girls help my mom and Willow get that first doe dried and cured. With the weather getting colder, I think we can freeze any of the meat we take from here on out. I almost wish we had snow. I really am tired of eating dried meat," Wyatt said with longing in his voice.

"Amen!" Jack agreed.

"What about Greg?" Wyatt asked.

"Why don't you have him help Chase with the border enforcement. The guy is an old Vietnam vet. He has some really good ideas," Bryan offered.

"Hey, if you guys do take a deer, Greg has been telling us he knows how to tan the hide. Maybe we can figure out how to make mittens, moccasins or other useful items?" Evan volunteered.

Wyatt got excited. The last deer they harvested had been quickly processed. He knew nothing about how to preserve the hide. He had felt like it was wasteful, but didn't want it laying around and attracting wolves or other predators.

Jack got excited. "I'm sure my mom and wife can figure out what to do with the hides once they're ready. That would be great. I'm guessing if we can get it figured out, the hides or items we make will be great for bartering, too."

"Sounds good. Any other strengths or skills that we can put to work?" Wyatt asked the two men.

They shrugged, "Not off hand, but you never know what someone can do until you ask."

"I think we should make some of those cold frame boxes Brenda was talking about. If we can grow some fresh root crops all winter, it will certainly help add to the food supply," Wyatt stated.

Evan nodded in understanding, "Those are pretty easy to make. That's a job that Earl can certainly handle."

"How is Earl?" Wyatt asked.

When they had first encountered him and the rest of the group, the man had looked to be in bad shape. Brenda had declared him to be relatively fine, just a little banged up. His arm had been wrapped. Wyatt hadn't seen him this morning. That was odd.

He made a mental note to seek the man out and introduce himself. If the man was going to be living at the lodge, he wanted to have a good feel for him.

"Okay, well, I think we got a pretty good plan for the day. Jack, what kind of lodgings are you planning on throwing up?"

Jack looked thoughtful for a moment, "I think the best option would be a longhouse. It wouldn't be as big or as fancy as they had in the old days, but we can make it so it's big enough to sleep eight or so. It only needs to be a bunkhouse. No point in adding windows and all that. Not now, anyway."

"Do we have the lumber?" Wyatt asked.

Jack shook his head, "No, but in one of dad's old books I'd read about how to hand hew logs for a cabin with a combination of mud and moss to create insulation. We have enough axes and man power. They won't be pretty, but we can make them work. I've already hewn most of that stack of logs I was saving to start one of the new cabins, so we can use them for the longhouse." He paused. "If we can swing it, we need to get busy chopping down some more trees so they can sit over winter."

Evan grimaced, "That sounds like a lot of work."

"It is," Wyatt stated with firmness. "If we're going to make this work and we want to plan to live here for a while, we need to be busting our butts. We are going to kill each other if we all have to live in this lodge for the next six months."

Evan groaned, "I've heard this area has long winters, but six months?"

Wyatt nodded, "On average. Maybe five months, but it's gonna be long, regardless."

"You know," Bryan started, "I know things are stretched tight, but we may be able to help ease that."

"How?" Wyatt asked immediately. Bryan and Evan exchanged

a look, "We had a couple of stashes around the camp. McDaniels didn't find them. They're buried."

"What's in them and are they worth going back for?"

Both men quickly said yes in unison.

"We've got more food, ammo, some medicine and even more guns," Bryan said.

"I don't know, Wyatt. It's risky. We have a lot of work to do here and going all that way, risking our lives and leaving the lodge vulnerable...I don't like it," Jack said.

"We are kind of desperate here, Jack. Any food and supplies we can get our hands on, we need to get. It's a small risk. We will leave enough people here to guard the place. With as many people as we have now, it's not a big deal if a few of us head back over there," Wyatt reasoned.

Jack didn't look convinced, but nodded in agreement.

"We go tomorrow," Wyatt said.

"Sounds good to us. First light?" Bryan confirmed.

"Yep. Let's get as much done today as we can," Wyatt said standing. "We are up against a tight timeline."

The men all headed out to hand out the assignments for the day. Wyatt was going to have to tell Megan about their planned trip tomorrow. She was not going to be happy.

Wyatt headed inside. His mom and Tara had the venison laid out on the counter. There was a ten-pound bag of salt out as well.

"What are you doing?" he asked.

Tara was using a cup to pour salt over each piece of meat.

"Curing the meat. We didn't get that smoker built, so Tara is showing me how to cure meat with salt and a few of the dried herbs we have," Rosie explained.

Once Tara poured the salt mixture over the meat, Rosie rubbed it in and then flipped it over. They repeated the process with each piece of meat.

"We cleared out an area in the shed, so don't be surprised if you go in there. We will be hanging the meat in there to dry," she explained.

"Isn't that going to make it salty?" he asked, trying to understand how that could be healthy.

"Not as much as you would think," Tara explained. "You could technically make a sandwich with it. We have sliced it thin. The salt dries out the meat faster than if we just hang it out there. With the cool weather, we need it to dry fast enough that bacteria won't grow. The salt speeds it all up."

"You have eaten cured ham," Rosie told him. "It's basically the same thing. It may not be as fancy a cure recipe, but it will do."

Wyatt was skeptical, but he was open to give it a try.

"Let me know when it's ready. I'll give it a taste."

Rosie laughed, "Oh you will most definitely be eating this, young man. If I serve it, you will eat it."

Wyatt had to laugh. It was the same thing she'd been telling him since he was old enough to eat. It was no surprise she still said it.

Chapter Eighteen

Jack had no idea if it was going to work, but he figured it wasn't going to be a complete loss. If the hewn logs didn't work out, they could still use the wood to burn during winter but then everyone would be on top of each other in the lodge.

He took a deep breath and swung the ax again. He had recruited Bryan and Evan to help him finish up the remaining logs. Jack figured he should give them a hands-on demonstration on how to hew their own logs.

"Are you sure you know what you are doing?" Evan asked just as he was about to swing.

Pointing to the stack of logs he'd already completed. "They didn't grow that way. Now quit talking to me while I'm swinging an ax or one of us is going to lose a leg."

He was frustrated and on the verge of losing his cool. This wasn't easy work; it required not only raw power, but concentration too. That's when he saw Megan walking towards them.

"What's up?" he asked, thankful for the interruption.

She smiled. "Not a thing. I wanted to see you in action. Wyatt told me you were hewing logs. I wasn't paying attention when you were working on them before so thought I would check it out. Why are you doing it? Can't you leave them round to build the longhouse?"

He sighed, "Yes, but imagine stacking blocks and then imagine stacking something like toilet paper rolls. It is easier to work with square pieces of lumber than the round logs. This way we can also make beams for the roof support."

She didn't look convinced.

"You could do that with the round logs as well."

He sighed, "Why do you think the pioneers took the time and energy to hew logs? They did it because in the end, it provided them with a sturdy building and a few guys could do it versus trying to put different sized round logs on top of one another."

"Okay, okay, I get it. You're right. Can I help?" she asked.

Jack knew Megan was very capable, but this work was extremely strenuous. He looked at her face. She wanted to help. He groaned inside. She was truly like a pesky little sister always wanting to tag along with the boys.

"Fine. You can use that ax. There is a smaller log already set up. You are going to score the log first, which is basically making a V shape about every foot on the log. Like this," he said picking up the ax and whacking it against the log he had started on.

The ax cut was about two inches deep. He swung again on the other side of his cut several more times.

"See the V shape?" he asked all three of his now attentive pupils.

They all nodded.

"Okay, keep making these deep Vs along the log."

He swung the ax a few more times, deepening and widening the groove. Then he moved down the log a foot and started the process again.

"You guys do the Vs down the length of your logs. When you're done, we'll move on to the next step," he instructed.

None of them talked as they got busy swinging and chopping. Despite the chill in the air from the cold breeze, sweat dripped down Jack's brow and down his back soaking his shirt. While he appreciated the cool down, it drove him to keep pushing through the burning in his arms.

It wouldn't be long before that breeze turned into a biting northern wind. They had to get this building up. He was hoping the hewn logs were worth the time and effort. He felt like they would be, but one just never knew.

"Done," Megan said breathlessly after spending close to an hour working on her one log.

Jack looked over and checked that the entire length of the log had the cut grooves down the whole length.

He smiled, "That is pretty amazing, Megan. You surprise me more and more each day."

Megan beamed. She was obviously feeling proud of herself as well. Bryan and Evan finished their logs up soon after and Jack gathered them all round again.

"Okay, now, you're going to chop the area between your Vs to make it all the same depth across the log," Jack explained.

He quickly went to work showing them how to shave off the center piece between each of the grooves.

Megan, Evan and Bryan quickly got busy doing the same. The sound of chopping wood echoed across the area. It was a cathartic sound making Jack feel like he was doing something useful and necessary. He was making a difference.

He finished his log and looked over to inspect Megan's. She was just finishing the last bit. Her face was red and he could see how much energy she was putting into her work. Not many women would be excited to hew logs. She was certainly unique. Wyatt was one lucky man.

She was a little out of breath when she asked, "Now what?"

He smiled, "How about we take a minute to catch our breath and drink some water."

"Fine, but I want to get this done."

Jack shrugged, "You're going to repeat everything you just did on the other three sides."

Megan groaned, "Ugh, for some reason I thought we only needed one side."

He laughed, "That would be an awkward beam. Probably not real effective either," he winked at her.

"Shut up, Jack," Megan said, playfully rolling her eyes.

They were all just finishing the last side of their logs when Wyatt walked up to their little log hewing party. Each of them was exhausted after hours of backbreaking labor.

"Wow, you guys have been busy," he said with admiration in his voice.

Megan used her forearm to wipe her brow, "Yeah. This is not an easy job."

"Is this all we need to do, Jack?" Evan asked.

Jack smiled. It probably looked like an evil smile to the three that he had been pushing so hard.

"Actually, not quite. It isn't as important as the actual hewing, but we need to run the ax head down the length on all four sides to kind of smooth it out. It doesn't need to be perfect, but we want them fairly flat so they will lay flush on one another."

"So, how long is this going to take?" Evan asked.

Jack pulled out his notes and began calculating. "We've already cleared the area where the longhouse will go and laid out the floor. If we work in teams, some building the house while others finishing hewing the last of the logs, we should be able to knock it out in a couple weeks. Month, tops."

"That long?" Megan asked.

"For the finished cabin, afraid so. Unless we can get more people working on it *and* work faster."

A collective groan came from the group. Wyatt shook his head, "I think you're enjoying this a little too much."

Jack laughed, but didn't deny it.

"So, I talked with Chase and got everything squared away for tomorrow," Wyatt said, directing the statement at Jack as well as Evan and Bryan.

"What?" Megan asked, stopping her work.

Jack grimaced. Wyatt hadn't told her. He knew she was not going to be happy. She would want to go along, but Jack was with Wyatt on this one—it was too dangerous. He didn't want to see her get hurt or worse.

"Uh, we, well, they," Wyatt stammered, gesturing to Bryan and Evan. "They, uh, have some stuff hidden at their cabin. We are going to get it."

She held her ax at her side, put her free hand on her hip and tapped her foot while glaring. Jack was always amazed at how women had perfected the I'm-going-to-skin-you-alive stance.

Jack grinned. He loved watching Wyatt get in trouble. Always had, even when they were little. Wyatt was a bit of a golden boy. It was good to see him be human every now and again.

"Megan, it's best if you stay here. It's too danger—" Wyatt stopped when Megan lifted her ax.

She used the ax to gesture at him, "I know you weren't going to say too dangerous, Wyatt Morris. You know darn well I have been doing nothing but dangerous for months. I'm still alive."

Jack thought about helping Wyatt out, but figured he had his own battle ahead with Willow. Big brother was on his own.

"Megan, that's not what I meant. Chase wants you here. He is counting on you to keep an eye on things here while he is out on the property with Albert."

Jack watched Evan and Bryan's reaction. They all knew Wyatt was saying they didn't trust the newcomers and wanted to keep an eye on them, not to mention the constant threat of a McDaniels' attack.

Bryan looked at Jack, then Wyatt, "It's cool. We understand. We would do the same thing."

Megan ignored Wyatt and went back to using the ax to smooth

out the beam she had created.

Jack and Wyatt exchanged a look. They both knew she wasn't happy. Jack decided he would talk to her before they went in for the night. Hopefully she would listen to reason and understand why it was best for her to stay behind.

He was very fond of her and certainly didn't want her angry or hurt by his decisions. The supplies were a necessity, but the trip would be extremely dangerous. Wyatt would never forgive himself if Megan was injured or killed.

Chapter Nineteen

"Clear?" Wyatt asked Bryan who had just joined the group after going back to make sure they weren't followed.

"I didn't see anyone. I think we're clear."

"Okay, let's go then. Keep your eyes and ears open, just in case they're hiding out around here," Wyatt warned.

They broke through the trees and Wyatt sucked in a deep breath at the sight before him. He kept expecting to see the gazebo and the new cabin they had built. But there was nothing but piles of smoldering rubble.

Jack stood beside him, "Oh, my God."

Wyatt turned to Bryan and Evan. Both men looked stricken.

Their camp was absolutely destroyed. There was literally nothing left standing. Now, Wyatt understood why they had made the journey to the lodge. They didn't have any other options.

"Let's go. I don't want to be here a minute longer than we have to," Evan stated moving to the tree line that shielded the main cabin.

Wyatt braced himself. They had said the larger cabin had been destroyed as well.

Again, the sight as he broke through the trees was far worse than he could have ever imagined. He felt as if he had been punched in the stomach.

There were clothes strewn about among the charred pieces of lumber. The Raiders had clearly looted the cabin before burning it to the ground, but there were still so many items wasted. McDaniel's Raiders weren't simply raiding to survive, but for fun too. The trees around the cabin were scorched. It was a miracle they hadn't started a forest fire.

Wyatt's sight focused on four small crosses in the middle of the scrap pile. It suddenly felt hard to breathe. He couldn't catch his breath as he imagined this same scene unfolding at the lodge. He imagined the screams of terror.

That little girl, Amy, had already seen so much. She had completely withdrawn, startling at any loud noise. After seeing something like this, he couldn't imagine how she would ever smile again. The blank stares and the reserved emotions from the newcomers all made sense.

They all had to have PTSD. One didn't come through something this horrible and not suffer any kind of mental trauma. Wyatt decided he was going to be a lot more patient with the people back at the lodge. They needed compassion and understanding right now. Not his distrust and scrutiny.

Jack put a hand on his shoulder, "We won't let this happen at the lodge."

Wyatt nodded, inhaling through his nose. The dead were buried, but in his mind, he could smell the death. It was a scene he had heard, smelled and been through more times than he cared to share during his time in the service. He never thought he would see it right here at home.

"Let's get the stuff," Bryan said. He walked further up the hill, behind the area where the large cabin once stood. He was looking up at the trees and then down at the ground. Wyatt assumed he was looking for a marker.

"Here. You two start digging here. I'll find the next area."

They worked fast and uncovered all four of the buried caches of food, medicine and a few SKS rifle coated in cosmoline and sealed. Every firearm they could get their hands on would make it a little easier to defend themselves against McDaniels. After seeing the devastation, he understood what Evan and Bryan meant when they said the man was unhinged.

There was no reasoning for what he had done here. The man was an idiot as far as Wyatt was concerned. The cabins could have been used by his men. There was no justifying burning perfectly good homes to the ground.

"I think we're done here. Let's head back," Bryan said.

Wyatt imagined he wanted to get away from the place that held such bad memories.

"I'm real sorry about what happened here," he started. "I want you to know you and your people are welcome at the lodge. I know things were a little rough yesterday, but we'll make it work."

Evan looked over the area, shaking his head, "Such a waste. It was all so pointless. They got very little. They are bad, bad men. We can't live in fear. We have to do something."

Bryan ran a hand over his face, "We can't live like they aren't going to find your home, Wyatt. I can guarantee they won't stop looking until they do. We won't be safe until every one of them is dead."

"We can't wage war against an enemy we can't find," Jack said.

Wyatt looked around again, "I guess we better find them before they find us."

The men left the camp and walked at a fast pace. After seeing the ruins of the camp, there was a sense of urgency to get home.

*　　*　　*

The lone figure watched as the men dug up the sealed cases. He knew there had to have been more. McDaniels should have listened. He waited and watched as they divided up the bags of jerky, medicines and the guns. They would need those weapons soon, he thought, chuckling to himself.

He followed the men as they walked at breakneck speed through the forest. They had clearly traveled this route more than once. Keeping his distance so as not to be detected, he left small markers to help him find his way back.

The sun was setting. If they didn't get to where they were going quick, it would be hard to follow them through the dark forest without them noticing. Just when he thought he was going to have to give up and go back, they crossed a small stream. Voices from above greeted them.

They had watchers in the trees. Good to know. He wasn't going to get across the stream without them noticing. He decided to go upstream and then try to cross. By the time the large lodge came into view, the sun was almost down. He could see men milling about talking and inspecting what appeared to be the start of another cabin.

A beautiful woman came out of the house and walked slowly to one of the men that had been at the burned-out cabin a few weeks ago. She wrapped her arms around him and kissed him. That was yet another piece of information that would come in handy.

It was easy to bring a man to his knees when the woman he loved was threatened.

He watched for a few more minutes before fading into the forest. It was a long hike back, but his adrenaline was surging. He had found them! This information would certainly earn him a spot at the table with McDaniels.

Chapter Twenty

Megan leaned against the pillows propped up against the headboard. It felt good to sit and relax. Wyatt laid next to her, reading an old Western novel he had found on the bookshelf. It had been a busy day for them both and they had decided to retire to the privacy of their room earlier than normal. With so many people milling about, it was hard to relax.

"You think we should go out again tomorrow?" she asked, carefully pulling the needle through the old baseball skin.

He shrugged, "Probably. One deer isn't going to last long."

Their hunting trip had been a success. Megan was excited to give the bow another shot tomorrow. She had missed today, but Garrett had managed to take one. He had given her plenty of pointers on how to aim the arrow slightly upwards before releasing the string.

Tomorrow was going to be the day she got her own deer with the bow.

"You think that's going to work?" he asked referring to the ball she was attempting to make.

"I don't know yet. It won't be as hard as a softball, but it will be okay, I think. Probably better for the kids anyways."

She pushed another old rag into the opening of her old softball skin. She was hoping the ball would be durable enough to hold up to a wooden bat.

"Caitlin really wants her own ball. This is my lucky skin. I had always planned on giving it to her one day. Now she can have it on her very own ball."

She continued to stitch around the opening. The silence was truly golden. She loved that they could just sit quietly without having to talk constantly.

With all the extra help the past few days, the workload was much easier to handle. The stash of dried beans, jerky and other food the men had brought back had provided a nice cushion. Megan didn't feel nearly as worried as she had a few days ago.

This was going to work. She had been hesitant, but it wasn't as bad as she had thought. Rosie had been taking the kids into the forest and foraging for any remaining berries. Willow was making jam with the berries, which she declared would be delicious on all the biscuits they would be feasting on throughout the winter.

"Done!" she declared, holding the ball up and turning it over in her hand.

Wyatt put his book down, "She is going to love it. Is the big game tomorrow?"

She nodded, "I think that would be good. We'll go hunting in the morning, take care of what needs to be done and then have a ball game. It will be good for all of us. Those guys need a little joy in their lives."

Wyatt had told her about the ruins and Megan's heart went out to Tara and Amy. She wanted them to feel welcome. Amy needed to do normal things like play ball with other kids.

"We need to mix up the teams a bit. I don't want it to be us against them. That's only going to divide us," she said thoughtfully.

"Good plan. Let's get some sleep so we aren't dragging our butts around the bases tomorrow."

She laughed, "You will be dragging. I am as fast as lightning!"

"Sure, Flash Gordon, sure. Goodnight."

*   *   *

Everyone rushed through their morning chores the following day. There was a lot of buzz around the lodge about the upcoming baseball game. Rosie and Willow were preparing an old-fashioned barbecue to eat after the game.

The old manual meat grinder had been pulled out. The fresh venison was being ground up. It was a two-man job cranking the

165

grinder. Tara was busy making buns and a potato salad—without the mayo. It smelled and looked delicious with lots of fresh herbs tossed in with the olive oil. The traditional potato salad would not be missed with this replacement.

The excitement in the camp was palpable. Everyone laughed and actually seemed excited to get their chores finished. Even the kids were more than happy to stack firewood, with Ryland taking on the chore of splitting tiny pieces of kindling.

"Mom, we're all done. Is it time yet?" Caitlin asked, hopping from one leg to the other.

Megan was just finishing up cleaning the outhouse area. With so many people in the lodge, it was painfully obvious they were going to need to build another outhouse and fast, before the ground froze.

"Almost, sweetie. I think Wyatt went out to get Albert and Brenda from their watch posts. He should be back any minute. Did you find those old pieces of carpet?"

"Yep, me and Amy got them all set up, just like you told us. We have all the bases and a place for the pitcher," she said with pride.

"Wow, you really are ready to go. Okay, go tell everyone to meet on the ballfield in fifteen minutes for our first softball game."

Caitlin looked at her, "It isn't actually a ballfield, mom. We just moved some stuff and put the bases down. I think it is pretty small."

Megan laughed, "Well, it is our ballfield and that is all that matters."

Once she was finished with the outhouse, she walked quickly back to the lodge to clean up. Rosie had filled the breakfast bar with stacks of fresh buns, lettuce and they actually had a bottle of ketchup. Sandra had thinly sliced potatoes and cooked them in the oven to create baked potato chips. Two fresh apple pies were also set out.

A plate of sliced squash was sitting at the end, ready to be put on the grill. Grilled squash was one of her favorites. A stack of grilled corn drew her attention. They didn't have butter, but they wouldn't need it. The food was going to be the main event.

It was going to be a real feast and Megan couldn't wait to dig in after the game.

"Did you make the score board?" Megan asked.

"Amy and Caitlin did earlier," Rosie told her. "This is a really great idea, Megan. It's just what we all needed."

Tara smiled, "Thank you so much for doing all of this. I haven't seen Amy happy in a long time. This is all so fun. It feels so normal to have a big barbecue. I can't believe we have hamburgers. My mouth is watering at the thought of biting into one of those!"

"Me too. It has definitely been a while. Funny how it's those little things you miss," Megan answered.

"Okay, well, if you ladies are finished, let's head out and get this game started."

Duke barked. He was just as excited as everyone else. He raced around in circles in front of Megan. His tongue lolled as he wagged his tail in excitement.

"You better come out with us, mister. I don't want you tearing into those burgers before we get a chance."

He barked again, his tail wagging furiously.

"Fine, I will let you have a little bite of mine, but that's it," Megan rubbed his ears to help lessen the blow of being denied a hamburger.

"Hey, you guys ready?" Wyatt called out opening the back door.

"Yep. Did you get Albert and Brenda?"

He nodded, "They were hesitant, but I told them they can play an hour or so. We have gone much longer in the past with no one on watch."

"Okay. Did you get the team roster?" she asked. He had taken on the task of dividing up the group into even teams, with players both new and older lodge members on each team.

He smiled, "Yep and you are not on my team so you better watch out."

She rolled her eyes, "You forget I was an All-Star. You don't scare me a bit."

Jack met them on the edge of the field, "You sure about this?"

Megan gave him a quick hug, "It's fine, Jack. We have to have some fun. This is going to be good for everyone. It's only an hour."

Jack looked at Wyatt, who silently begged him with his eyes to let them enjoy this one little piece of normal.

"Okay, but don't go crying to my mom when I beat your batting average."

Megan giggled and took off running towards her team that was already lining up in the outfield.

"Don't you go crying to her when you get beat by a girl. Both of you!" she shot back as she took her place on the pitcher's mound.

Megan took a moment to breathe in the fresh air. She missed this. She missed standing on a pitcher's mound. She missed being carefree. She took a moment to look around her. Everyone was talking and laughing.

This was perfect. They would give themselves an hour to unwind before they had to go back to their chores and responsibilities. She was going to treasure every moment they had doing totally normal things, like playing ball. It was something she had taken for granted in the past, but never again.

Chapter Twenty-One

"You're out!" Greg, acting as umpire, shouted at Bryan who had just missed touching the base before Wyatt caught the ball at second.

Megan danced on the pitcher mound. Her team was up by two and victory was in her sights.

"Remember Wyatt, no cry—"

Her taunt was interrupted by the sound of gunfire. It was a semi-automatic weapon. No, her brain registered...it was several semi-automatic weapons.

David who had been at first base fell face forward into the dirt. Screams erupted all around her. She stood on the pitcher's mound in complete shock. Oh my God, no.

Wyatt's hand was quickly on her own, dragging her towards the lodge.

It was then that it all clicked. They were under attack. Men were coming out of the trees, spraying bullets.

"Caitlin! Caitlin!" she screamed, tugging against Wyatt's grip to find her daughter.

"Mom has her. They ran for the lodge already. Megan, we have to move!"

Megan raced behind Wyatt as fast as her legs would carry her.

"Get in position! Everyone, get in position!" Wyatt screamed over and over.

Through the chaos, Megan saw people scattering in different directions. They had talked about what they would do if they were attacked. It looked like everyone remembered.

Wyatt threw open the mud room door and pushed Megan in ahead of him. "Get up there, Megan. Take out as many as you can!"

She nodded and raced through the lodge. She saw Rosie shutting the secret door in the kitchen and prayed Caitlin had made it into the safe room.

She took the stairs two at a time. Her corner was waiting. She grabbed the gun that had been put against the wall for this exact reason. It took her less than a second to dislodge the wood they'd placed in front of the hole they'd made and got the barrel into position.

Megan took a deep breath, peered through the scope, found a target and pulled the trigger. He dropped.

She quickly reloaded, slid the bolt action into place and looked through the scope. She spotted Jack in hand-to-hand combat with one of the raiders. She hesitated. If she fired and missed, she would hit Jack.

As she watched the two men fighting, she saw Jack throw his head back in pain before putting a hand on his leg. The brief pause in the fighting gave her the window she needed. She took the shot. It hit the man in the shoulder, causing him to drop the knife and retreat.

It would have to do. Megan quickly reloaded and looked for another target. A bullet slammed into the outside wall next to where she was standing. It didn't come through the wood, but it was enough to scare her.

She realized too late her position could easily be compromised if she didn't crouch low. The idea was for her to remain unseen. Sticking the barrel of her gun out the hole in the wall wasn't smart. She waited a few moments before carefully peering out the slit.

It appeared they were all retreating. She wanted to take out as many as she could before they fled to safety.

Another shot and another man dropped to the ground, just before he got to the safety of the trees.

She reloaded and looked through the scope. There was no movement. She scanned the area.

Wyatt was crouch-running to Jack who was limping towards the lodge. He put his arm around Jack before shouting. She couldn't hear the words, but she could tell from Wyatt's expression this wasn't good.

He looked directly at her, even though he couldn't see her, and waved. The attack was over.

Megan slowly pulled the barrel back in and replaced the gun in its designated corner. Her legs were shaking and she didn't know if she could walk on them. The surge of adrenaline that had driven her up the stairs had left in one swift whoosh. Now, she was left feeling shattered and empty.

She slowly walked to the stairs. Gripping the handrail, she made her way back down forcing her legs to take each step. Her eyes saw the flurry of activity as people ran around grabbing towels and blankets. There was blood all over one man who had been laid out on the kitchen table. The table where they were to enjoy their feast. How could everything go from perfect to disaster in a flash?

Wyatt came through the door, supporting Jack. He dropped him in a chair at the breakfast bar before running towards the secret door.

Rosie, Willow and the kids slowly walked out.

Megan stood at the halfway point on the staircase, watching everything unfold. It reminded her of watching one of those old silent movies. She could see mouths moving, but she heard nothing.

"Megan? Megan, are you hit?" Wyatt was standing right in front of her.

He grabbed her face with both hands, "Did you get shot? You're bleeding. Where are you hit?"

"What?"

She heard his words, but surely she hadn't been shot. She didn't feel any pain. She was numb actually.

He turned her head to the side and then turned her around to look at her back.

"I think you were grazed by a bullet. Looks like it went right by your ear. You have a small cut above your ear. Mom will take care of it. Come on, we need to check for wounded."

He grabbed her hand and started to pull her down the stairs. She didn't move.

"Megan, we need to take care of the others."

He said the words firmly and in a way that cut through the fog in her brain.

She blinked several times.

"Wounded. Got it. Let's go."

She followed him down the stairs, watching Brenda try in vain to save David who was lying lifeless on the kitchen table.

Wyatt walked over to his mom and gently pulled her hand away from the man's bleeding stomach.

"Brenda, there are others who need you right now. He's gone."

Megan stared at the dead man. Her mind refused to accept what was unfolding. She looked at Jack who had a dishtowel pressed to his thigh. It was soaked in blood. All the food was sitting on the center island. It was a stark contrast to what was happening all around the kitchen.

"Mommy," Caitlin whimpered. "Mommy, I'm scared."

Megan looked over to see Caitlin standing against the wall by her bedroom door.

"Oh baby, I'm so sorry. I'm so sorry. Don't worry. It's all going to be okay."

Amy was curled up on the floor next to Caitlin. Ryland was doing his best to soothe her. Frankie stood off to the side. There was a blank stare on his face. The kid had seen far too much death and destruction.

"Ryland, I need you to take the girls upstairs. You know where my gun is, right?"

The adolescent stood tall, put his shoulders back and nodded, "Yes, ma'am."

"You take them up there and if you hear anything down here, you get them into your mom's bathroom. Take the gun. Shoot anybody that tries to get through the door."

Ryland nodded. "Got it."

"Thank you, Ryland. I appreciate you being so brave. Caitlin, Amy, you girls follow Ryland and do as he says."

She turned to Frankie, "Frankie, can you please help Ryland? I need you to keep being brave."

The little boy looked at her, his bottom lip quivered, "I will. I can be brave." He looked down at his feet. "But, I'm really scared."

Megan wrapped her arms around him, "It's okay to be scared. We're all scared. Stick with the others and we will make sure no one gets in here, okay?"

Frankie rubbed the back of his hand across his eyes, "Okay. I'll be brave. Please hurry back, though. I don't want to be alone."

"Oh, honey. You won't be alone. You see all these people here? They're all going to be right here. If you have any problems, you go see that guy," she said pointing to Chase who was essentially directing traffic.

"Okay," Frankie replied, after a big sniff.

"Alright, go on upstairs and we will all be back soon."

"Megan, let's go," Wyatt said from the door.

She quickly walked to the door and took the .45 he handed her.

"Just in case they aren't all gone," he told her.

She hoped they weren't all gone. She wanted to shoot them all.

Albert was outside the mudroom door, leaning against it. Blood was trickling down his arm.

"Albert, were you hit?" Wyatt asked.

The man shook his head and used his other arm to wave him off. "Not my blood."

"Anyone else out there who needs help?"

Albert looked away, "Sandra, but she didn't make it. I tried to get her inside, but it was too late."

Megan gasped. "No!"

Wyatt cursed.

"Get inside. My mom will check you over just to be sure. We're going out to see if anyone else needs help."

Wyatt and Megan walked towards the ball field.

Tara stumbled out of the trees from where she'd been hiding, "Amy?" her voice was barely above a whisper.

"She's fine. She's upstairs with the other kids," Megan assured her. "Are you okay?"

Tara nodded, "Ya, I took off running at the first sounds of gunfire. I got to my weapon, but I froze."

She looked mortified and her head dropped in shame.

"It's okay, hon. It's over now. Head into the lodge. They could use all the help they can get in there," Wyatt told her in a soothing voice.

They continued walking. Bryan and Evan were knelt over one of the men Megan remembered shooting. It was the man who had been fighting Jack.

"Is he dead?" Wyatt asked.

"Yep. Just getting his gun and ammo."

Wyatt turned to look at Megan, "You?"

She nodded. Seeing the man lay dead in front of her should have bothered her. The bullet had hit him in the chest. It was a perfect shot. That was what she focused on rather than the fact she killed a man.

Megan noticed the man's bloody hand. The knife he stabbed Jack with was laying just a few inches away.

The knife handle had blood smeared on it, as did the blade. But it wasn't just blood she saw. It was rust and what appeared to be dried blood. The man had stabbed Jack with a rusty knife.

"He stabbed Jack with that knife," Megan said, looking directly at Wyatt.

Wyatt looked at the knife and grimaced.

"I'll let Brenda and my mom know. If Brenda stitches him all the way up, it will definitely cause a serious infection. As it is, we need to make sure she loads him up with all the medicine she can find."

"I hit another one too," she said, looking around the area, already switching gears. "There was another guy around here."

She didn't want to panic, but if he had gotten up, she would be very mad at herself. She had thought she delivered a kill shot. Maybe she was wrong. Bryan stood, "We already took his gun. He's over there. Clean shot to the head." He was very serious, but gave her a quick smile, "You are a hell of a shot, Megan. I'm glad we're on the same side."

"Thanks. I just wish I could have gotten more."

The group started walking back to the lodge, "Is everyone accounted for?" Evan asked.

"Yes. David and Sandra are dead," Wyatt swallowed hard. "Jack was stabbed. There are a couple of other minor injuries, but nothing that won't heal."

They walked in silence. Each of them caught up in their own thoughts.

"We better get busy digging graves. Is there anywhere in particular you want them?" Bryan asked.

Megan was shocked at his all-business demeanor, but then remembered they had been through this several times already.

"Man, I hadn't even thought of that. I don't want it close to the lodge," Wyatt said, rubbing his face as he thought about it.

"How about on the far end of the garden? That area under the trees," Megan suggested.

Wyatt nodded, "That works."

"We'll grab the shovels and get busy. Maybe have someone prepare a speech so we can get this over with. The sooner we put this behind us, the sooner we can move forward," Bryan stated, his tone emphatic.

"I didn't know David at all. Maybe one of you? Tara will probably want to take care of the eulogy for Sandra," Wyatt told them.

Megan could see it was weighing on him.

When they left Bryan and Evan, she grabbed him and pulled him in for a bear hug.

"It wasn't your fault. Don't try to shoulder all the responsibility here," she told him.

He squeezed her tight, "I should have known better and left

someone on watch. I was naive to think it would all be okay. It was a mistake I will never make again. We need to get someone out on watch, right away. They could be out there right now, reloading and preparing for another attack."

She shook her head as they headed back to the lodge. "I doubt it. They ran out of here pretty quick the second we started shooting back."

"We can't take that chance. I need to get out there and scout the area."

"Wyatt!" Willow shouted. She stood in front of the back door holding a few bandages and gauze pads.

"What is it?" he asked, quickly making his way to her.

She pulled him away from the mudroom and was talking in a low voice. Megan watched and waited. Wyatt would tell her soon enough.

A variety of emotions crossed his face—shock, anger and ultimately devastation. Megan quickly stepped inside and scanned the room to take a head count. She didn't see Duke. Had they killed Duke? His bark from upstairs had her smiling with relief. Everyone else was accounted for.

Megan wasn't going to wait. She had enough surprises for one day.

"What happened? What is it?" she asked.

Willow looked at Wyatt, "He'll tell you. I need to help get Jack patched up."

Wyatt grabbed her hand and pulled her toward the root cellar.

"They wiped us out!" he said angrily.

"What? When? How?" she asked not believing it was possible.

"They had to have done it before they opened fire on us."

She followed him, stealing a look at the goat pen to make sure they were both in the pen and alive. When she saw the two kids dancing around as if nothing had happened, she breathed a sigh of relief. Megan turned to see Wyatt crawl into the root cellar. She could hear him cursing as she climbed down behind him.

The shelves were nearly empty. All the food they had been preserving was gone.

Megan stared at the shelves in shock. How could they possibly survive without food on the brink of winter?

"This stays between us for now. If we tell everyone what happened on top of what just happened up there, there will be panic."

Megan felt sick. The attack was horrible, but this was devastating.

"What are we going to do, Wyatt?" she whispered. "What will we do?"

He didn't answer her. He just looked around the storage that had been ransacked. Broken jars littered the ground. The men were savages.

"Let's get out of here. We need to take care of our wounded. We will deal with this later."

She didn't push it. He needed time to think and process. She understood. For now, they would take care of those that were injured and clean up what they could.

Chapter Twenty-Two

"It could have been much worse," Jack murmured from where he sat propped up on his bed.

Under Brenda's careful supervision, Rosie had stitched the long gash in his thigh, but left a small area at the end open. Brenda had been teaching Rosie more of the technical side of medicine. It was unfortunate that this was the perfect time for her to get some hands-on training. The goal was for everyone to know a little bit of everything instead of a lot about one thing.

Rosie had placed the tube of a ballpoint pen in the hole so it could drain once the infection started to fester.

"Are you sure this will work?" Rosie questioned.

"I have done it a hundred times."

It was a trick Brenda had picked up in the field. She had used what she had to clean the wound as best as she could, but she had made it very clear she would prefer something more powerful than soap and water.

They knew it was only a matter of time. Rosie had covered the wound with raw honey, but that wouldn't do much for the toxins that had gotten into his bloodstream. It was a watch and wait situation. Wyatt didn't want to think about the worst-case scenario. No point in borrowing trouble.

"Yeah, it definitely could have been," Wyatt agreed.

Evan had left once they got Jack situated. The brothers needed some privacy.

"If they hadn't been here—Evan, Bryan, Garrett and the rest— we would have easily been overrun. I don't think McDaniels' men would have left any survivors," Jack stated matter-of-factly.

Wyatt winced. It was something they had long feared, but to have witnessed the destruction the men were capable of first hand was a huge eye opener.

He blocked images of Megan standing on that mound, exposed. How the bullets missed her was beyond his comprehension. He hadn't taken the time to analyze the situation.

"I think I counted five men armed with those AR-15s," Wyatt said.

Jack nodded, "Yeah, I don't know for sure. It felt like there were twenty men shooting. Everywhere I looked or ran, there were bullets flying."

"How long do you think they were out there?" Wyatt asked, not really asking Jack, but merely speaking what had been on his mind all day.

Jack leaned back and looked at the ceiling, "Probably all day waiting until we pulled the guards in and started the game. Our guard was completely down. We were completely exposed. Quite frankly, I probably would have taken advantage of the situation as well. We messed up."

His words were exactly what Wyatt had been thinking. They had been spied on and they didn't even know it. He had no idea if the men found them by chance or whether they had followed Evan's group back. Maybe they had followed them back on the quick supply run they had made.

There was no point in wasting energy trying to solve that mystery. What was done was done.

Wyatt stared at the wall, "They know where we are. They know where our supplies are. They are going to come back."

Jack nodded, "It's a guarantee they will be back. I didn't see McDaniels. This was probably just a small raid. He's going to come back in force. I don't know if we'll be quite so fortunate the next time around."

"We have to do something. Winter is fast approaching and the only food we have is what we brought back from Evan's camp and that won't last long with the number of mouths to feed. This is probably the absolute worst case scenario."

Jack agreed, "Talk with Bryan and Evan. See where their heads are. I am up for anything. It may be a day or two to let this thing heal, but I'll be back on my feet in no time."

"Okay, well, get some rest. I'm sure Willow wants to spend

some time with you. I need to go get everyone settled down. See in you in the morning."

Wyatt walked through the lodge, taking a few moments to chat with everyone. Evan was taking watch at the lodge. Brenda insisted on pulling a double shift and keeping watch in the bird's nest Albert usually occupied so he could get some rest.

Wyatt doubted anyone was going to get any real sleep tonight. Tension was high. Everyone was scared. He knew some of the new members were reconsidering their choice to join the lodge. They had better make their decision whether they were going to stay or go real quick.

They couldn't afford to have anyone stick around if they weren't in it to survive and overcome.

Megan had already retired to the bedroom. When he walked in, she was sitting at the foot of the bed, holding the softball she had made for the big game. Now instead of a source of happiness, it would be the cause of bad memories for years to come.

He hated that something she had loved so much was forever tainted.

"I don't know why I saved this skin. I think it's cursed."

He knew she was referring to her friend falling in the well all those years ago and now what happened today.

"Bad things happen. We knew something like this could

happen. We were basically ready for it."

She shook her head, "We let our guard down. I encouraged this big game. It cost two people their lives. Jack was stabbed, others were shot. It was a disaster."

"Stop, Megan. I need you to dig deep and find that anger. Find that resolve to push through, even when things are really tough. I know you have it in you. You have proven your strength time and again."

She gave a weak smile, "Maybe I'm tired of having to prove it all the time. Can't we just catch a break?"

He chuckled, "That would be too easy."

He sat down next to her pulling her in close. "We'll get through this."

"I think they attacked because the other group came here. They left us alone this whole time and now they attack?"

Wyatt was afraid she would blame the others.

"They would have found us eventually, regardless. The difference is we probably wouldn't have survived had Evan, Bryan and the rest of them not been here to help us fight back and defend the lodge."

She didn't look convinced.

"Seriously, they would have easily overpowered us. We didn't stand a chance against them."

"I guess, but it is odd they showed up today after leaving us alone all summer."

Wyatt put a hand on her knee, "They showed up because they were searching harder. They've already raided everywhere close to them. They're expanding their search to have enough to get through winter. Their desperation is obvious."

Megan bunched her fists up tightly, "I want to kill them all. It's burning like a fire in my belly. I don't think I have ever been one to wish death or want to kill people, but right now, that is all I can think about. I want to wipe them off the face of the earth," Megan said with vehemence.

Wyatt completely understood how she was feeling. He was feeling pretty violent himself at the moment.

"All of those traps we set. Why didn't those stop them?" Megan asked.

He shrugged, "We hadn't completely closed in the perimeter. Maybe they went around or maybe some did get caught in the traps. I don't know. Tomorrow I'll investigate."

"I think we need to attack right away. They are back there at their camp, eating our food and celebrating what they did. They won't expect us to show up at their door, prepared to kill them all. McDaniels needs to be our main target. We take him out and the rest will disappear."

Wyatt appreciated her fervor, but it was too soon. They weren't ready.

"Megan, we don't even know where to go."

"I do," she said hopping off the bed and finding the map she had carried with her to Evan's camp in the past. "You see this small clearing. I am confident this is where they would have set up their camp."

When he looked at her, questioning her assertion, he saw the anger burning behind her eyes.

"I was right about Evan's camp. I am right about this one!"

She had a point.

"Okay, but we need to get in some basic training. You are talking about going to war, and we don't have an army. Leaving the lodge vulnerable isn't an option. We need trained fighters here and there."

She nodded her head. He could tell she thought she was ready. One could never really truly prepare for war. Granted they had seen some pretty rough stuff today, but that was nothing compared to what she was talking about.

"We'll need to get everyone else on board. I have a feeling some of them aren't going to be okay with us heading headfirst

191

into a battle," he told her gently.

"Fine, then they can live in fear. They can live their lives constantly worried if today is the day they are slaughtered in their own homes."

Wyatt stood up and stripped off his shirt and jeans. He was beat. He wanted to close his eyes and forget the day ever happened.

"Megan, we'll talk with everyone tomorrow. There is no point staying up all night, fuming and stressing out. Let's go to bed. I need to sleep."

She watched him crawl under the covers. At first, he thought she would argue with him.

"Fine. I guess. But I am not going to let anyone talk me out of this. I will not sit here and wait to be killed. I will not put my daughter in that position."

She quickly stripped down to a t-shirt and crawled into bed next to him. Wyatt pulled her in close, cherishing the quiet moment between them. After the day they'd had, he wanted to savor these moments. He wasn't convinced they would have many more.

Chapter Twenty-Three

Megan woke early and judging from the tension in Wyatt's body, he was already awake.

"Ready for this?" she asked.

He didn't answer her. She waited.

"I'll talk with the guys. You talk with Rosie and Tara. Jack will need to talk with Willow. I think there is going to be some resistance to our plan."

"Should we just have one big group meeting?" she asked, hoping to cut out a lot of the talking and get right to the doing.

"No. That will create chaos. Everyone will want to talk and it will be counterproductive to what we need to get done."

She sighed. He was right—again.

"You do realize we can't go racing over there today, right?"

Megan considered punching him in the ribs.

"Yes, I know that, but I don't want to wait too long. The longer we wait, the more prepared they will be or they may even attack again."

"I agree."

He sat up and they both quickly dressed in silence. Megan noticed dried blood on her arm. It wasn't hers. After yesterday's events, she needed a bath. She'd been too tired to think about it last night, but today was different. She needed to wash away the blood and the bad memories it brought back.

They quietly walked into the kitchen. It didn't appear as if anyone else was up yet. Megan took a moment to look around the lodge. There were people everywhere. Sleeping bags and blankets were spread across the floor near the woodstove. With Jack laid up, it would be up to the rest of the group to finish the longhouse he had started.

Evan and Bryan came in the back door. Their cheeks were pink. She could tell they had been out walking around. The cold air clung to them.

"Hey," Wyatt said in greeting. "All good?"

Bryan nodded, "Yep. We just did a quick sweep of the perimeter. It was clear."

"You guys want some hot tea?"

Both men nodded eagerly. Megan figured they were probably pretty cold; the chill of winter had certainly arrived. They had insisted on sleeping in that stupid tent and she knew the temperatures were dropping to the freezing point at night.

"What do you guys want to talk about?" Evan asked.

Megan was only a little surprised he knew they had something to discuss.

Wyatt grinned, "You know us too well."

"After yesterday, I know you guys are itching to make something happen." He looked at Bryan, "We're up for it. We are ready to rid the earth of these scum."

"Good!" Megan said a little too eagerly. "I'll grab the map. Wyatt, no tea for me. I am about tea'd out," she said rushing to the bedroom.

Megan dashed back into the room and headed for the table to spread the map out. She used a red pen to mark the area she believed McDaniels and his raiders were holed up.

"You sure?" Evan asked, scratching the side of his head.

She was getting tired of people asking her that.

"Well, I don't have a guarantee, but it makes sense. When they pulled out the map that day, I noticed Xs on your camp and Brenda's. I am assuming those are camps they've hit. There was a red circle area—no X. To me, that says base and the Xs say target. You said it before; they have to be in that general vicinity."

"Okay, I get it. I'm game. What do you think? A day's hike?"

Wyatt nodded, "Yes, but with these short days, it's going to be a lot of hiking in the dark. That alone could be tricky."

"But it will help conceal us. The dark is actually a good thing, for us anyway," Megan pointed out.

"She has a point," Bryan added. "I like the idea of hitting their camp at night, scoping things out and then attacking at first light when they will all be half asleep."

Megan had to hide her excitement. They were going to do this. The plan was being formulated and she couldn't wait to see those men die. They had caused so much grief and pain; it would leave the world a better place if they were eradicated.

As the rest of the lodge woke up, each person was informed of the plan. Some people were hesitant, but in general, everyone was excited at the idea of living a peaceful existence without constantly worrying about being murdered in cold blood for no reason.

Albert and Greg had asked for a few minutes of Wyatt's time. Megan was invited to join the conversation as well.

Albert looked uneasy.

"What's up?" Wyatt asked.

"We would like to get all of the kids up to speed on shooting. There are four of them. That is four more guns pointed at the bad guys."

Megan's knee-jerk response was a resounding no.

"Hell no," she clarified her initial answer.

"Megan, think about it. These kids are not living in typical times. I would never, ever think about training a child to shoot another human, but this is different. Their very lives may depend on it," Albert explained.

It made her sick to her stomach to think of her little girl shooting and killing a person. It would strip away that innocence that all children should get to hold on to for as long as possible.

Wyatt looked thoughtful.

"I think you're right," he said. "Caitlin and Ryland already know how to shoot. I'm not sure about Amy and Frankie, but it would be smart to make sure they can each use a weapon."

Megan looked at him in shock.

He turned to her, "Megan, you have to think about what may happen if you or I or all of the adults are injured or killed. Do you want to leave the kids vulnerable? Obviously, we wouldn't be sending them out to the front lines, but if there is an attack here again, they need to be able to defend themselves."

"I know what you're saying, but I know how bad it messed me up after I killed Kyle. I can't imagine any one of those kids having to go through those emotions."

Greg shook his head, "Times are different. They've already seen more than a typical adult would have a year ago. I think it will give them confidence. We don't want them feeling anxious or scared. If they know how to use a gun and where to shoot to stop someone from hurting them, I think it would go a long way toward making them feel better."

She slammed a fist on the table, "I hate this, but fine. Yes, please teach my daughter how to be a little soldier."

"Megan, you know it isn't like that. You have to be on board with this or she is never going to do it," Wyatt reasoned.

"Fine. I will talk to her and let her know I need her to do this."

Greg stood, "Great, we'll get started on it today. We don't have time to put it off."

Wyatt looked pensive, "I think we should also teach everyone here, especially the women and kids some self-defense. I showed Megan some moves a while back and they came in handy."

Megan nodded. Oh yes they had. She had managed to disable Kyle Grice and save her life and the life of her daughter. She absolutely wanted Caitlin to know how to escape anyone who tried to take her or got close enough to harm her.

"I'll go talk to Jack. See how he's doing while you guys get your training classes organized," Megan said leaving the table.

"See if the kids are up and moving yet. We'll be out at the ball field cleaning things up and then set up some targets for them," Albert said.

"I will. Thank you guys for doing this. I can't say I am thrilled with the idea, but I do understand how important it is," Megan said making eye contact with Albert and Greg.

They both smiled and nodded before heading out the door.

*　　*　　*

Megan tapped on the door to Willow and Jack's room.

Willow swung it open. Her eyes were puffy and Megan could tell she had been crying.

"Hi, come in. I'm going to get breakfast started," she said before rushing past Megan.

Megan walked to the bed where Jack was laying. His face looked red. He had a fever. It was evident he was in some pain.

She put her hand on his forehead, "I'll let your mom know."

"Don't bother. Willow woke her up hours ago. My mom gave me one of her magic teas. It was to be expected. My body has to fight the infection. It's not a big deal, Megan. I can fight this; Willow is just super sensitive after everything that has happened."

Megan didn't blame her. She wasn't exactly chipper when Wyatt had been laid up. His injury was bad, but Jack's was already showing signs of an infection.

"What's up? When are we attacking?"

She laughed, "How'd you know?"

He rolled his eyes.

"Because I know you and your blood lust and I know you would have convinced Wyatt to exact some serious revenge."

"Well, you know we have to do something."

He nodded, "Yep, and don't you dare think I am going to sit in this bed while you guys go off on a crusade. I'll be right there, taking out as many as I can."

Her gaze fell to Jack's thigh, "We'll just have to see about that."

Megan quickly told him about their plan to attack within the next few days. She explained the self-defense training everyone was going to go through and the shooting lessons the kids would be getting.

"Ryland will do great. He is a good shot. So will Caitlin, of course. I hope Amy isn't too young."

"I don't think her age matters at this point. We aren't going to have them packing, but if it gets desperate, it will be good to know they can pick up a gun and fight back."

Megan couldn't believe she was defending the very idea she had just argued against.

"Get some rest, Jack. I want you there by my side when we

kill that vile man."

"I will. Thanks for coming by."

Megan headed out to find Wyatt. She wasn't entirely sure what she was supposed to be doing today. There was a nervous energy racing through her veins in anticipation of going to battle. This was probably not a big deal for Wyatt or Chase, but for her, this was huge.

Wyatt was talking with Tara and Willow. Both women were nodding their heads, looking nervous and excited at the same time.

"There you are," he said when he spotted her walking towards them.

"What's up?"

He winked at her, "I need you to be my victim for our little self-defense class here."

She laughed, "The chance to knock you on your butt, you bet! I wouldn't miss it!"

Megan and Wyatt worked together; setting up three different sessions to ensure everyone had a chance to learn the moves. When it was time for the kids to go through their lesson, Megan worked with Caitlin. She wanted her daughter to feel comfortable with hurting another person if her life depended on it.

That night at dinner, the mood was very subdued. There was no dinner conversation. No kids teasing each other. Even Duke was very mellow choosing to lay by the fire rather than his usual place at the table, where he waited for scraps to fall.

Immediately after, everyone who wasn't on guard duty headed to bed. The tension in the air was thick. Megan didn't completely trust all the new members and she imagined they were feeling the same thing. Their fates were tied together. If they weren't on board with the plan to attack, it wouldn't work. They needed everyone working together.

She decided to talk to Wyatt about it once they were alone and everyone else was asleep.

"Do you think all of the new people are really okay with our plans?" she asked.

He shrugged, "If they're not, they should leave. I think tomorrow we will need to talk with each person. Get an idea of where they stand. Bryan and Evan will probably have a better idea about their people, but I want to judge for myself as well. I don't want a bunch of lip service."

Megan was relieved he was on the same page.

"So, do you think we're ready?"

He thought for a second, "I don't know that I would head out to take out a top terrorist, but I think we can get it done. We have surprise on our side, which is always going to be a good thing. They won't expect us to take the battle to them."

She breathed a sigh of relief. If he was confident, she was confident. They could do this. They could fight back and win.

Megan prayed the cost wouldn't be too high.

Chapter Twenty-Four

Megan shivered as she stood on the bank of the stream, drying herself off as best as she could before pulling on her shirt. Thankfully, they were going straight back to the lodge or she would spend more time making sure she was completely dry before dressing to avoid losing too much body heat. She had taken a quick sponge bath the day before, but she hadn't been able to shake the feeling of being dirty. She wanted a bath—a cleansing bath.

It was far too much effort to fill the tub upstairs and with so many people in the lodge, it felt weird. When she had complained to Wyatt, he suggested a dip in the stream. It would be ice cold, but she didn't care. Or at least she didn't think she would care, but after a few minutes, the icy water proved to be too much.

"You are going to freeze to death in there!" she scolded Wyatt who was lazily splashing around in the water.

"It gets your blood pumping. It's invigorating," he yelled back.

"No, it freezes your blood. You're going to have hypothermia."

She focused on putting on her clothes as fast as she could. The warmth of the sweater she had been wearing quickly took off the chill. The gun Wyatt had brought along with them was sitting on the top of his clothes.

They were close to the lodge, but he didn't want to risk being unarmed.

Splashing and heavy breathing behind her alerted her to Wyatt's trek out of the water.

She watched him striding towards her. He was freezing. He would never admit it, but his skin was bright red and the way he moved told her he was feeling that prickling sensation that happened when a person was overly cold.

"Hurry up. I want to go stand by the fire now."

"You are the one who said you wanted a bath. I was just trying to accommodate," he said with a wink.

"Bath and plunging into a stream of ice are two different things."

He laughed, "Well, now you know. You have to admit it really wakes you up."

She nodded, "Yes it did. But now I really want a fire. And hot chocolate. With marshmallows."

"I can get you a fire, no can do on the cocoa."

He picked up his gun once he finished dressing and they headed back towards the lodge.

Megan relished the feeling of clean hair. Pouring a cup of water over her head was not the same as washing her hair. The cold water had left her scalp tingling, but it felt great.

"Shh," Wyatt said, suddenly pulling her behind a large tree.

Megan's heart skipped a beat and then began pounding so hard it hurt.

"McDaniels?" she gurgled, barely able to form the word.

He shook his head. They both waited and watched.

Earl was skulking through the trees. He kept looking behind him. Wyatt gestured for Megan to stay put. They watched him for a few moments before Wyatt mumbled that he had enough.

"Earl, right? You're Earl? I don't think we really got the chance to talk," Wyatt said walking out from behind the tree with Megan following close behind.

Earl froze. The look on his face revealed how shocked he was.

"Um, yeah, I'm Earl. I came in with Evan and Bryan."

Wyatt nodded his head, "Yep, I remember. You were injured and my mom took care of you."

Guilt was written all over the man's face and Megan knew that was what Wyatt had intended.

"So, where you headed?"

Earl looked around, as if he hoped to escape or fade away.

It was then Megan noticed the folded paper in his hand.

"What's that?" she said pointing to the paper in his hand.

Wyatt reached out and snatched it from him.

As soon as she saw it, she knew what it was. It was the map they had used to identify where McDaniels was camped.

Wyatt raised an eyebrow and Earl looked like he wanted the ground to swallow him.

"I don't suppose you were planning on taking on the whole gang yourself?"

Earl slowly shook his head. "No."

Wyatt nodded in understanding. Megan didn't get it. What was Earl going to do?

"You were hoping McDaniels would let you join his group. You provide them with information about our planned attack and maybe where our traps are located in exchange for him letting you join them?"

Earl's head dropped and his shoulders slumped forward.

"I hate to admit it, but I'm tired. I'm scared. I don't want to die. You have to know you can't beat them. If you can't beat them, join them, right? That's what my dad used to tell me. I'm just doing what I think is the smartest thing."

Wyatt looked furious.

"So you thought selling out the people who took you in was a better choice? Evan and Bryan took you in. They trusted you enough to bring you here and I trusted them. Now you are going to get my family killed to save your own skin?"

Megan was furious. What kind of man betrayed the people who looked out for him? Sheltered him. Fed him.

Earl shrugged, "I don't know what to say man. I'll go back, but I'm not going to help you fight McDaniels. That's a death sentence."

Wyatt looked thoughtful. He looked at Megan and then back at Earl, "How about you just go on your merry way. I'll keep this map and you can keep whatever food you stole."

Megan looked at Wyatt with shock. He was going to let the man go?

Earl nodded, "Thanks, man and uh, sorry about all this. It's nothing personal, I need to look out for myself, you know?"

"Yep, you sure do. Bye, Earl."

Earl turned and hurriedly walked towards the perimeter. Megan watched in disbelief.

She was about to ask Wyatt what he was thinking when he pulled the gun out from his waistband. He didn't stop to think about what he was doing. He aimed and pulled the trigger.

Earl dropped.

Megan's mouth dropped open.

Wyatt looked at her as he tucked the gun back into his waistband, "Him or us. Quite frankly, any man that would willingly put his life above women and children doesn't deserve to live."

Megan stared at the dead man. He had fallen onto the ashes and bones leftover from the pyre where the rest of McDaniels' men had been burnt. The pyre was meant to deter anyone else from trying to come after them.

Striding over, Wyatt pulled the pack off the dead man and slipped it over his shoulder. "Let's get back. We need to have a talk with Bryan and Evan. If there is a chance any of their other people want to leave, I want to know now."

Megan didn't answer. She didn't know what to say. Wyatt just shot a man. He didn't seem bothered by his actions at all. He was all business.

They walked back to the lodge without saying a word and Megan was surprised when she saw people hiding amongst the trees near the lodge, guns at the ready. After hearing the gunshot, those on watch had been in position, prepared for an attack.

After settling everyone back down, Wyatt tracked down Bryan and Evan who were working on the longhouse that Jack had started. Megan saw Jack trying to help as well.

She gave him a look.

"I'm fine. I'm not swinging an ax; I'm only running the ax down the logs they've hewn. We can't afford to have anyone sitting on their butts right now."

Wyatt told the three men what had just happened.

Megan imagined the look on Jack's face mimicked her own when it had happened.

"I'm sorry about that," Bryan said. "Earl was one of the more recent additions. We hadn't gotten a chance to know him all that well before we were attacked. The guy he showed up with was killed in the attack and he was injured. I guess we didn't think of him as a threat and that's on us. We should have been more cautious."

Wyatt nodded in understanding.

Megan imagined Earl had probably been scared out of his mind. He was so focused on saving himself, he couldn't see how much danger he was putting himself in, let alone the rest of them.

"Needless to say, is everyone else solid? Garrett?" Wyatt asked.

Both men vehemently nodded their head, "He is a good guy. Solid. Has always been willing to help out and when we were attacked, he saved little Frankie. I will vouch for him," Evan stated.

"Okay, then. Well, hopefully that was our last defector. Are we going to be ready to move in the next day or two?"

Jack looked down at his leg, "I'm going with you. If you can give me a day or two, I'll be good as new."

Bryan and Evan both nodded in agreement.

"To be on the safe side, we'll give ourselves five days. We have five days to get our people armed and ready, just in case our attack is unsuccessful. Every one of those men will be out for blood if they escape."

Chase joined the group, "We'll be ready. We're making a wall of pikes right now. I have the boys working on sharpening some of those small downed trees into sharp points. We'll be using rope to tie them together to create a gate of sorts."

"Won't they just go around them?" Megan asked a little confused on how that would be effective.

Chase smiled, "The gate will be under some branches and dirt. They won't know it's there until it springs up in front of them. It will be the only open entrance to the lodge. There will be pikes, barbed wire and various traps along the rest of the perimeter. They will naturally go for the area with the least resistance."

Wyatt looked impressed.

"Good thinking. Very medieval, but smart. I like it."

Wyatt gave him the rundown about the situation with Earl. Chase was equally disturbed by the idea the man would have betrayed them all if Wyatt and Megan hadn't happened upon him in the woods. The outcome would have been disastrous.

"Alright, we are going to get busy. See you all tonight at dinner," Wyatt said, grabbing Megan's hand and heading into the lodge.

Chapter Twenty-Five

The day started out with a flurry of activity. Wyatt and Megan were going out to scout for a bug out retreat, just in case McDaniels' men managed to breach the perimeter and get close to the lodge. If things were looking bad, they needed an emergency escape plan.

Brenda insisted she go along. She had been all over the mountain and knew the area fairly well. She hadn't found anything around her house or towards Evan's camp, but there were still plenty of areas to explore.

"How about you and Chase go up the mountain a bit. Megan and I will go towards the west," Wyatt decided.

Chase agreed, but felt they could do more.

"Why don't we send Garrett and Greg out, too," he suggested.

Megan agreed. The faster they found this secondary location, the better she would feel. Even if it only offered a breather for the group to recuperate until they could retake the lodge. She hated the idea of running blindly through the forest. She had been there, done that and didn't want to do it ever again.

"Okay. Let's set a time to be back. Everyone sticks together. If a group doesn't come back by three, we know something went wrong and can put everyone at the lodge on alert. Agreed?"

A chorus of agreements rang out.

"Alright, get your packs and let's get moving," Wyatt said, anxious to get started.

Everyone quickly checked the gear in their packs and headed out in their respective directions.

Megan and Wyatt hadn't found anything and were ready to call it a day when they saw a trail of rocks ahead of them.

"A path," Megan said squatting down low.

She used her hand to brush away pine needles and some of the overgrowth.

"Look!" she said, pointing to the rocks that were in a neat little row. She brushed away more needles and brush and found what she was looking for. It was another trail of rocks.

"This is a path to somewhere," she said in an excited voice.

Wyatt stood between the two lines of rocks and looked ahead. Wherever these rocks led was obscured by the trees.

He walked forward, kicking branches and thorny bushes as he went.

Megan rushed to get right behind him, literally on his heels. When he came to an abrupt stop, her face hit him in the back.

"Megan, we found it. We found the bug out location!"

Megan pushed him out of the way so she could see. It was a small hunting cabin. It wasn't exactly big. In fact, she was pretty sure it was about the size of one of those tiny homes that had been so trendy before the EMP hit.

"Well, it's a cabin. I don't know how we are going to squeeze seventeen people in there, even if we all stood shoulder to shoulder," she said not sharing his enthusiasm.

"It's better than nothing. We can always build on. The idea is somewhere to run to. Honestly, if we are sending anyone here, it's because our numbers have been depleted and we can't fight back. The survivors will fit just fine."

The realization of what could happen over the next few days was sobering to her. She could die. Wyatt could die. The time they had right now mattered. She wanted to make the most of every minute.

"Let's check it out," she said pushing him forward.

There was a small stick threaded through a latch that was holding the wooden door shut. Not exactly the most secure place, but she pushed out the negative thoughts. If the other two groups hadn't found anything, this was their best and only option.

Wyatt opened the door and popped his head in.

"Holy crap!"

Megan didn't know whether to be scared or happy.

215

"Holy crap!" Wyatt said again.

"What? What is it? What's wrong?"

He grabbed her and pulled her in. "Look!"

Megan's eyes adjusted to the dark interior. She blinked several times before finally focusing on a glass gun cabinet in the corner of the room. It was filled with rifles. There were three crates stacked next to the gun cabinet; all labeled in block letter with the word "Explosives".

Along with the guns and ammunition, there were several five-gallon buckets along the edge of the wall.

"Do we dare open those?" Megan asked. "What if they are poop buckets?"

Wyatt chuckled, "Not every bucket is a poop bucket."

She didn't look convinced.

"I don't know," Megan gestured around the room. "Rustic cabin, no bathroom, you do the math."

"I'll open one. If it's poop, we know, but what if it's ammunition or food?" Wyatt asked.

"I'll wait."

Megan stood near the door. She had accidentally opened one of the poop buckets at the lodge not knowing what it was. She was scarred for life.

Wyatt pried up the lid on one of the buckets.

"Well, it isn't poop," he said. "It's beans. A lot of beans."

"Check the other two," she ordered. She wasn't totally appeased.

"Ammo and," there was a pause, "Sugar or salt. Hold on," he said. "Sugar."

"That's awesome. With our food store being raided, sugar will be a welcome addition. Should we take what we can carry and come back tomorrow to get the rest?"

He nodded, removing rifles from the cabinet and handing them to her.

"We'll take these for now along with some of the dynamite. Tomorrow when we come back, we'll look around for any other supplies. We will need to have a small stockpile here, just in case."

Megan felt a huge weight lift off her shoulders. At least they had an option if the lodge was compromised. It wasn't as nice or stocked, but it was better than sleeping under the trees.

As they walked back to the lodge, Wyatt talked about how ironic it was they were looking for a bug out location. The lodge had been their bug out location and now they were very possibly going to have to leave it behind. A bug-out for their bug-out.

"I'm so glad you know about all this stuff. I never would have thought to find a backup home. I guess I've always been in the mindset to take it as it comes. I have to start thinking like you. Always thinking about the future and playing out the various scenarios. You are very smart, Wyatt Morris."

He turned and kissed her.

"Thanks, but it isn't being smart. And really, it was all my dad. He was always telling us to plan for anything and everything. His motto was prepare for the worst and hope for the best. I have tried to keep that mindset. I think I kind of forgot."

Wyatt told her he knew not to get complacent. He knew survival situations were fluid. They were constantly evolving. They had been comfortable in the lodge, but if they had to move, that was fine. All he needed was his family. He could figure out the rest later.

Right now, he wanted their focus to be on getting through the coming week alive and Megan couldn't agree more.

Chapter Twenty-Six

Wyatt was hoping Brenda and Greg would be able to get the rifles in working order. He could see they were old and it was hard to say how long they had been sitting in that cabin; although judging from the amount of dust, definitely years. Brenda had proven her ability to dismantle, clean and fix firearms more than once. She was probably the closest thing to a firearms expert they had.

"Wyatt. Megan. I'm so glad you are both back in one piece," Rosie greeted as they walked through the back door.

He stopped abruptly. The kitchen smelled amazing. He looked around and saw a huge spread of food.

"Mom, isn't this a bit…extravagant?"

She smiled, "Sometimes you need a good meal with good company to overcome hard times. We didn't get to enjoy our big barbecue feast. The group needs this," she said the last part so only he could hear.

Taking a deep breath in, his mouth instantly began to water followed by the rumbling of his stomach at the smell of roasted turkey. While they had been eating turkey off and on for the last month, this was different.

Megan pushed him out of the way, "Oh my goodness, Rosie!

When did you do all of this?"

The woman smiled, "We have had those pumpkins sitting out there, waiting to be canned. Willow and I got the idea to make some fresh pumpkin pies. Then Garrett returned with three fresh turkeys and the idea popped in our heads. Thanksgiving!"

Wyatt had forgotten about the holiday. It didn't seem all that important in the grand scheme of things. After the raid, he wasn't sure there was a lot to be thankful for.

"This is amazing, guys. You really outdid yourselves—I cannot wait to have some pumpkin pie," Megan said eyeing the pies cooling on the counter.

"What do you have there," Brenda asked walking towards them.

She was eyeing the rifles like a kid in a candy store.

Wyatt smiled, "I got you a little project, Brenda. You think you can check these out and see if they are functional?"

She reached for the rifles, fixated on them.

"Yes. Absolutely. Thank you."

Wyatt raised an eyebrow. The woman was a bit of a strange duck.

He figured he better clarify what he meant.

"I'm hoping they all work. There are a few more back at the

cabin we found. If we can get them all functioning, there will be enough for every person here. With seventeen people armed, we stand a pretty good chance of defeating any army."

Greg took one of the rifles and began inspecting it.

"Winchester model 94 .30/30s and some bolt action .30-06 and .270s. What do you think, Brenda? Can we handle the job?" Greg asked her.

She didn't seem to hear him, as she turned and walked upstairs carrying the guns pressed against her chest.

Greg laughed, "I'm gonna take that as a yes." Turning back to Wyatt and Megan, "I'll go put this upstairs and after dinner we will get to work."

"Did anybody have any luck finding anything?" Wyatt asked the room in general.

Garrett answered, "We found a small dam upriver. Nothing else, though."

Wyatt nodded. He had no idea there was a dam. It would certainly be a good idea to check it out once things settled down. Once the spring melt started, it wasn't unheard of for a dam to be breached. Things could get dicey.

Albert was sitting at the table, his leg propped up on a chair.

"Hey Al, I wanted to show you something. I need your expert

opinion," Wyatt carefully removed his backpack, being sure not to jar it.

He unzipped it and pulled out one of the sticks of dynamite he had taken from the crate.

"You think this is any good?"

Albert whistled low.

"Boy, what in the world are you doing with that?"

Wyatt smiled, "We found a crate full. Maybe it was used for blasting up here in the mountains. I don't know. You think it's any good? Like, can we use it to blow some bad guys up?"

Albert nodded, "I'm guessing you can blow up anything, including us if you aren't careful. That stuff is old. *Real* old. There is no reason it wouldn't explode."

He carefully handed the red stick back to Wyatt, "You best put that away somewhere real safe. You found a whole crate of it you said?"

Wyatt nodded. He could see Albert formulating a plan.

"And you found the blasting caps?"

Wyatt nodded, pulling out the pieces that would be put on the top of the dynamite and lit.

Albert looked impressed. "Those are fuse caps, which means we can light them and run. I think that would be a great way to get the message across to leave us all alone. You plan to take it to them?"

Wyatt hadn't thought it out.

"I'm not sure yet. We'll have to do some planning. I'm not sure I want to carry sticks of dynamite across the mountain."

"With this cold weather, it won't be too bad. How was the crate packed?

"Some sort of waxy cardboard," Wyatt answered.

"Did you see any crystals on the outside of any of the sticks?"

"Nope. Everything looked clean. Just dusty."

"It's a great find, Wyatt. You too, Megan. You all did good today," the old man praised as he smiled broadly. "Now that everyone is back, Rosie, are we gonna eat? I'm starving!"

"Oh, relax. You've been sitting there for an hour. We told you it wasn't ready yet," Rosie scolded, bringing plates to the table.

"Willow, will you round everyone up while I get everything set up. We'll just set it up as a buffet. Everyone will have to find a place to sit."

"Who's on guard?" Wyatt asked. He didn't want to take any risks. The last time they thought they could enjoy some time together with the entire group, it had gone very bad.

"Jack insisted," Willow grumbled. "His leg is not getting any better, but he said he could sit and watch."

Wyatt looked around the room to see who else was missing.

"Tara?" he asked.

It was Chase who came in from out back and confirmed his guess.

"With Jack. She needed to do it," Chase said with authority. "She has been feeling like a victim, understandably so. This will be good for her."

Wyatt didn't say anything. He wasn't sure an injured Jack and a fragile Tara were the best security choices, but so long as they were safely up in the bird nests with the ability to sound the alarm, he would leave it be for now.

"Let's go wash up, Wyatt," Megan said, grabbing his hand.

He followed her out the door. He knew she wanted to talk to him in private.

"What's up?"

"Is it safe to have Jack and Tara on watch?"

He grinned. They were on the same page.

"We need to make sure everyone feels valued. We'll let them do their part until after dinner, and then we will switch out the guard."

"Okay," she said, nodding in agreement.

The next hour was filled with a lot of laughter and banter. Brenda was joining in the conversation and appeared to be enjoying herself.

Bryan had asked Brenda about her time in the service. She started talking and everyone listened in awe.

Wyatt watched Megan as she made her way around the room, chatting with the lodge members she hadn't gotten a chance to know yet. She spent some time with little Frankie. He could see she was naturally drawn to the little boy.

Wyatt stood against the wall, eating his pumpkin pie, watching the scene. It reminded him of Thanksgivings past. His mom would always prepare a huge meal and invite people from the neighborhood. His friends and any other strays she could find were always welcome.

This was a lot like those days.

Evan stood beside him, "It's nice, right?"

"What?"

"People talking and getting to know each other. Breaking down some of those walls. Megan seems to be opening up to the idea of us being here," Evan stated.

Wyatt knew she had been standoffish in the beginning. It was no secret to them or the newcomers that she wasn't thrilled to have them at the lodge.

"She was worried. She doesn't trust easily, especially if there's any potential risk to her daughter. When she first got here, it took her a long time to warm up to us. Me, even," he said with such incredulity it made Evan burst out laughing.

"You! You don't say. I would have thought she would have fallen at your feet."

"You know what I mean. Give it time. She'll end up embracing you all—she's one of the warmest, kindest people I've ever met once you get to know her. I think once we take care of this other problem, everything will mellow out. We can get through winter and figure out how we are going to go about building a community."

Evan slapped him on the shoulder, "We will succeed. All of us have already lived through some pretty rough stuff. We got this."

The confidence in his voice was nice, but Wyatt wasn't all that convinced they would come out unscathed. He imagined there would be more losses before all of this was over.

He wasn't afraid to die during his two tours in Afghanistan or his time in SWAT; he knew death could come at any time. But now...now he wanted to live. He needed to live to keep his family safe and Megan and Caitlin were very much part of his family.

"You ready for bed?" Wyatt asked Megan.

She was standing against the wall next to him looking drained. Wyatt figured it was the socializing that wore her out more than the physical labor of walking to the hunting cabin. She didn't seem to be a social butterfly.

"I am. I'm beat. Are we heading back to that cabin tomorrow?"

"Yep. We'll take Evan and Chase with us. Bryan and Jack can keep an eye on things here. Albert is going to help Brenda and Greg get those guns cleaned up and in working order."

"Good. I feel better knowing everyone will have guns and if a retreat has to happen, the people here will know where to go. We need to use the compass tomorrow to give everyone an exact direction so they all know how to get there," she said.

He nodded, "Good plan. We'll try to track how far it is so they will know if they are close."

"How?" she asked.

"Ranger beads are really the only option. Hold on," he said opening the dresser drawer and pulling out a leather strap with a row of beads on it.

"What is that?"

"These are ranger beads, a tool used by the Army to help with land navigation. They're very easy to use. They just aren't heard of much anymore since GPS was so much easier."

She held the beads, rubbing them between her thumb and forefinger.

"So, all of the beads are at the top. When we start walking, we count how many steps we take. An average guy takes about sixty steps to travel one hundred meters. For every sixty steps, we pull a bead down. When we have pulled down twenty-seven beads, we have traveled about a mile."

She looked at the strand. "There are only twenty beads."

He nodded, "When you pull them all down, you start over, remembering how far you've already traveled. You can determine the distance you want each bead to stand for. We can use yards or miles, but it gets tricky remembering to count, especially when we travel through rough terrain. Our steps aren't going to be quite the same compared to traveling on flat ground."

Megan marveled at the beads, "Well, at least it gives us an idea. We can have the kids make a set of these for every person here."

Wyatt took the beads and put them on top of the dresser. It had been a long time since he used them. He had held on to them more for nostalgic purposes than anything else, but he was glad he had them now.

"Once they're made, we will have everyone attach the strap to their pack or on their jacket. That's how we wore them in the field."

Megan stood, kissed him and smiled, "You are full of surprises. Those are clever. I can't wait to try them tomorrow."

He laughed, "Don't thank me yet. Counting to sixty over and over gets old fast. You have to stay focused or you will forget what you're doing. When you are all alone, thirsty or hungry, the beads are great because they give you something to focus on other than your misery."

"I can see that."

"I just pray everyone will learn how to use them. Their lives may depend on it."

Chapter Twenty-Seven

"Watch your step," Megan instructed Caitlin. They had decided to take Caitlin and Ryland to the cabin so the kids would know where they would be running to should things go south.

The cabin didn't appear to hold any other bounty, but at least they had a point B to bug out to.

They had spent some time at the cabin, searching the area and looking for any surprises. Megan was worried there may be traps like Brenda had set. She didn't ever want to deal with that mayhem again. It appeared to be completely deserted and uninhabited.

It was exactly what they needed. They collected the remaining items and started the journey back to the lodge. The men were carrying the rifles and the dynamite, while Megan carried a container of the sugar and the kids carried the beans. They figured they would leave some of the food items at the cabin.

Wyatt explained that he planned on dividing some of their food stores once all of this was behind them. He wasn't going to risk their main supply being raided again. He was convinced there would be others like McDaniels, but next time, they would be better prepared.

"Wyatt! Wyatt!" Rosie was shouting, as they approached.

She was waiting outside the lodge as the group came from the west.

He picked up his pace and passed Caitlin and Megan who had been in front.

"What's up, mom? Is everything okay?"

Rosie was wringing her hands.

When the rest of the group caught up, Wyatt looked ashen. Rosie looked extremely distressed.

"What's wrong?" Megan asked, looking around to see if there were any signs of a recent attack, but saw nothing.

"It's Greg," Wyatt explained.

"What happened?" Evan asked.

"His heart. I guess he has been taking aspirin to head off a heart attack. He was on prescription meds before the EMP, but with no access, he's been relying on aspirin. It was all taken in the raid."

Evan looked shocked.

"I had no idea. I just assumed he had a lot of headaches. There isn't any other aspirin around here?" he asked.

"I have looked high and low. We have ibuprofen, but it isn't the same. He needs the aspirin. He was walking out to guard duty today and began to have chest pains. It scared me to death!"

Rosie explained.

Wyatt looked grim. That is all they needed. They couldn't afford to have such a solid guy go down. They needed him.

"Does Brenda have any ideas?"

Rosie shook her head, "No. She says aspirin is really the best option under the circumstances. Bark from a willow tree would work, but I haven't seen any around this area. They require a great deal of water to grow. If we had time, we could have someone follow the stream to look for some."

"We'll find some," Megan said with intensity. "He will be fine. We can find a willow tree right, Wyatt?"

Wyatt nodded, but she could tell he wasn't convinced.

They all walked back to the lodge. Greg was at the table with a couple of the rifles laid out but he was moving slow. His pallor didn't look good to Megan. He seemed pale. She could see a fine sheen of sweat on his brow and he was breathing hard with very little effort expended.

"How you doing old man?" Evan asked.

Megan could see Evan was fond of the guy. They all were. He was one who had reached out to her early on and made her feel at ease. He was a good guy and she couldn't imagine him dying.

They had come so far. Greg was one of the few people she

readily trusted. She just got that good vibe from him and had no reservations.

"Wyatt, can I talk to you for a minute?" she said gesturing towards the bedroom.

She shut the door behind him.

"We have to go now. We can't wait a week, Greg may die!" she hissed. "If we go roaming through the woods looking for a willow tree, we may be attacked. We just need to go and get the aspirin we know they took."

"Megan, we aren't ready," he said in a voice meant to soothe her. "You don't even know if we will find aspirin in the middle of a camp of mercenaries. It seems like a lot to risk to find a few pills, don't you think?"

It incited her. How could he not be worried about Greg?

"You don't get to be ready. We are ready enough! If we wait a week, they may attack us, Greg may die or there may be a snowstorm. Why wait?"

She was surprised when he didn't immediately shoot down her demands.

"Okay. I'll talk to Evan, Bryan and Chase. If they think we are ready, we'll go tomorrow. That's the best we can do."

Megan nodded, too shocked to say anything. She wasn't naive

enough to think she had convinced him with a few words. He wanted to go. She just gave him a good reason.

Wyatt turned and left the room. She couldn't tell if he was mad or going into soldier mode. He did look incredibly determined.

Megan plopped down on the bed and Duke jumped up and sat next to her, waiting for an ear rub.

"Am I being too hasty?" she asked the dog. "Am I actually ready to do this?"

A million thoughts crossed her mind. What if they failed? What if she was injured or killed? What if Wyatt or any of the other men were hurt? Worse, what if they were all killed and the lodge and Caitlin were left vulnerable? They were risking a lot for someone who up until recently was an outsider to the group.

Her heart started to race and she found it difficult to take a breath. She sat on the bed, trying not to let a full-blown panic attack overtake her.

Her vision started to blur.

"Just take a deep breath, relax."

Jack's voice reached her just as she felt herself spinning into a black hole. She concentrated on his smooth baritone voice, cutting through the blackness. Her mind latched onto the sound as if it were a lifeline.

She crawled her way back out, relying on Jack's steady voice to lead her.

"There you go. Slow it down."

He was rubbing her back. The weight of his body was pressed into her side. She leaned into it and let him support her.

"Feeling better?" he asked.

She nodded, "Yeah. That was kind of silly."

"No, it wasn't. Wyatt told me you want to move up the plan. You're having doubts. It's normal. What we are about to do isn't going to be easy. It's dangerous and I think it's good you have a healthy amount of fear and trepidation about it."

She smiled, "I definitely have that."

"Good. I don't want to go into battle with someone who thinks they are invincible. That will get us all killed."

She looked at him, "Are you sure you should go? You aren't looking so hot, Jack."

He leaned back and laughed, "Thanks. I'm fine. Just a little fever. My body is fighting the infection. I'll be okay. No way am I letting you all go into battle without me."

Megan looked at him. He didn't look fine. There was sweat on his brow. He didn't have a small fever. He was burning up. She could feel the heat radiating off him. He looked pale, but if he insisted on going, she wasn't going to be able to stop him. Hopefully, they would be able to find some antibiotics for him along with the aspirin. It was a tall order, but she had to stay positive.

They sat there in silence, each lost in their own thoughts.

Wyatt appeared in the doorway and Megan met his eyes.

"We need to talk."

Jack stood and Megan could see his leg shaking. She met Wyatt's eyes and saw he also noticed his brother.

Jack saw them both looking at his injured leg and waved his hand, indicating it was not a big deal.

"It's fine. A little weak, but fine. I need to stay moving or it gets a little stiff. I'll leave you two alone."

"No. We all need to talk. Everyone is anxious about the attack. We need to come up with a plan for there and here."

His gruff voice and cold demeanor alarmed Megan. She wondered if Wyatt was on board with the attack or if something else was bothering him.

Jack left the room, Megan waited for Wyatt to say something. He didn't.

"Wyatt? What's wrong?" she asked when he only looked at her—not speaking.

"We are headed into war, Megan. I would feel better if you stayed here. I don't think I can focus on the fighting if I have to worry about you. You don't seem to get how serious this is. This isn't a play war or something we can walk away from if it doesn't go our way."

She didn't get mad. Yes, she was a little offended to hear him imply she wasn't taking it seriously, but she had come to know him well enough. This was his way. He hated her being in danger and that fear usually came out as anger. She got it.

"I will take it very seriously and I am ready to take these men down. You don't have to worry about me. I will have your back and I know you will have mine."

He hugged her tight.

"Don't you dare get yourself killed out there. I don't think I could handle it."

"Same goes for you. We go in. We kick some butt, gather supplies, find the aspirin, and get on with our lives. Those guys will be nothing more than a bad memory."

"Let's go hash this out. Everyone is pretty freaked out. I think a lot of them thought this would all just go away. There are a few very unhappy campers out there," he said. The dread in his voice was easy to hear.

The next several hours were filled with lots of raised voices, a few tears and a lot of emotions as they all worked out the details of the raid.

It wasn't going to be easy and they all knew the chance of failure was high.

"We don't know how many people they have," Garrett pointed out. "We could take ten guys and end up facing fifty."

Megan rolled her eyes. The guy still hadn't accepted the fact she would be there. She was also wondering where he thought they were gonna find ten guys to take. Willow and Rosie certainly weren't going.

"There could be ten, there could be fifty but we have the element of surprise on our side," Wyatt explained.

"The dynamite isn't such a bad thing either," Albert pointed out. "A big explosion could level the playing field real fast."

"What about the guns?" Tara asked. "You haven't had time to get all the guns fixed. We won't be fully armed back here."

Willow spoke up, "I think a few guns left here will be plenty. The chances of us winning in a firefight are slim. We would have to run. I don't want to waste time shooting at people when we could be getting the kids to safety."

Jack agreed with his wife, giving her shoulder a quick squeeze.

"She's right. If we aren't successful, your main goal is to get to that bug-out cabin. Everyone has a pack ready to go. If you hear shooting, take your packs and get the hell out of here. No heroics."

Rosie was in the kitchen, preparing small lunches for the group traveling. She told them she needed to do her part and food was important. They had to have the energy to walk there, fight and get home.

She was using a large majority of their remaining food stores, but told them not worry, when they got back, they would replenish the food pantry.

Megan appreciated her optimism. She hoped it would all work out as planned.

After the long planning session, everyone was physically, mentally and emotionally exhausted.

They were leaving before dawn and the mood in the lodge was somber. All of them wondering if this would be their last night here. Would they ever all be together again?

Megan held Wyatt tight.

"We have to win tomorrow," Megan vowed.

"I don't know if there is any winning involved, but I am going to do everything in my power to ensure McDaniels dies and we all live," Wyatt promised.

Megan closed her eyes and tried to envision coming home after a successful raid. The vision just wouldn't come to her and she couldn't shake the sense of foreboding. She silently prayed it was only her nerves and not some intuitive sixth sense.

Chapter Twenty-Eight

The tension was palpable as the group prepared to head out into the morning chill. Megan was fighting back nerves and her stomach was in turmoil. Rosie had gotten up early and prepared a small breakfast for the group heading out, but Megan couldn't eat a bite.

They had tried to keep quiet to avoid waking up the rest of the lodge, but everyone was now standing in the dining area, watching as Wyatt checked everyone's packs.

Jack, Chase, Evan and Bryan had divided the dynamite between them.

Willow watched with tears in her eyes. Jack smiled to reassure her, but she just cried harder.

Brenda watched Jack with a careful eye. Megan wondered what was truly going on with his leg. She had a feeling Brenda knew. Jack probably knew, but he certainly wasn't saying. In fact, he'd been quiet the last couple days, which was very unlike the normally warm and talkative man she'd come to view as family.

Megan hugged Caitlin, praying it wouldn't be the last time. She wanted to remember every little detail about her baby. This would be what carried her through what was sure to be an extremely difficult few days.

"You take care of her," she told Albert, squeezing him tight.

"You know I will. You just get your butt back here in one piece."

The kids knew what was happening, but Megan hoped they didn't truly understand how serious it was. She didn't want them living in fear.

Rosie, Willow and Albert would each have a gun. The rest were to be used by the group heading to McDaniels' camp.

"Everyone ready?" Wyatt asked. Megan, Chase, Bryan, Evan, Jack, Brenda, Greg and Garrett answered yes in unison.

"Got the radio?" Albert inquired.

Wyatt would be carrying the portable HAM, just in case he needed to radio back to the lodge. If things went bad, Wyatt wanted to give Albert as much warning as possible.

Megan headed out the door. She turned back to take one last look at Caitlin who was standing next to Rosie. Her little girl smiled and waved. Megan waved back and followed the rest of the group blinking several times to push back the tears that threatened to fall.

She wasn't going to cry. This was not goodbye; it was see you later. She had to hold on to the idea she would be back and everyone would live happily ever after.

Here goes nothing, she thought to herself.

The group made good time, each of them taking turns supporting Jack. He kept trying to refuse the supportive shoulder, but they all knew he needed it. They didn't make a big deal out of it and it was almost like a dance as the next person simply stepped up and slipped their arm around his waist and continued walking without mentioning what was going on.

Megan looked back and saw Brenda and Jack talking as they walked. Their voices were too low for her to hear.

Brenda noticed her watching and quickly stopped talking. Megan had a feeling the good doctor was lecturing Jack about the journey.

They didn't bother stopping to eat. No one wanted to waste even a minute, adrenaline was pumping and they silently pressed forward. As they got closer to where they suspected the camp to be, everyone went on high alert.

Megan's stomach had been in knots. She could see the physical changes in the way everyone was walking and constantly scanning the area.

"Anything?" Evan whispered to the group.

"Nothing. Stay on your toes. We need to spread out. Walking in a single group is going to draw attention. Especially, if they have someone watching," Chase said. "Do what you can to stay single file; it's harder to see you like that, especially with all the trees."

They fanned out into groups of three, with Wyatt, Jack and Megan sticking together.

Megan's mouth was dry and the butterflies in her stomach worsened. Taking long, slow breaths, she was doing everything she could to keep from vomiting and they weren't even there yet.

Jack had been trying to keep her calm, but now he appeared completely focused on walking.

She had grown more worried about him the farther they went. He was walking with a pronounced limp and had lost almost all color in his face. His mouth was set in a firm line and she knew he was in a great amount of pain.

Wyatt stopped when they reached a dirt road, his brow furrowed.

"I know this area."

"Really?" Megan asked, looking around. There weren't any road signs or other obvious markers.

He nodded, "Yes, there is a big stone house up the road. Actually, it's just a small driveway off this road."

Jack looked around, "Yeah, didn't an old couple live up here? They were real secluded. I remember the house. Dad was in awe of it."

"What about the house?" Megan asked.

"It resembles a castle. A fancy castle, I guess you could say. It's huge. Way bigger than just two people needed, but the dude was mega-rich."

Wyatt snapped his fingers, "He was some dot.com guy. They moved up here from California. He sold his company for billions. He was always talking about a major financial collapse driving the country into ruin. If I remember right, he had a huge basement filled with food and water."

Jack nodded excitedly, "Yep. That is what spurred dad into stockpiling. Our stores are nothing compared to what that guy had. He went all out."

"It makes perfect sense McDaniels' would hole up here. It's secluded and plenty big enough for his gang and there was a lot of food."

Megan got excited.

"Maybe there is still a lot left? Once we kick these guys to the curb, we could gather the remaining supplies."

Wyatt agreed, but wasn't hopeful.

"They are raiding and taking food and other supplies. That suggests they already ran through whatever was in the house."

Megan felt deflated. For one moment, she imagined filling the root cellar.

"If we use dynamite, the supplies are going to be lost; if there are any left, anyway," Jack reminded her.

"We need to meet up with the others. I'm almost positive that's where they are. The house is about a half mile off this road. I say we scope things out and attack at dawn," Wyatt said, giving the signal to the others.

They had worked out different bird calls to communicate. They knew they would have to divide and conquer, but still needed to be able to talk with one another.

When everyone regrouped, Wyatt gave them the rundown. He explained his thoughts, but couldn't make any guarantee he knew where McDaniels was hiding out until they investigated. There was still a chance they were in the wrong place altogether.

They decided to head back down the road to make camp. They didn't want anyone from the other group stumbling upon them if they happened to be in the area.

They skipped building a fire. It was cold, but they didn't want to risk the smoke drawing unwanted attention. The last thing they needed was to be found and attacked when they were the intended aggressor. At this point, they still had the element of surprise on their side. To risk that now could well ensure their death sentence.

They built two shelters from green tarps.

"Let me get some pine needles down," Megan said when Jack made a move to crawl into one of the shelters.

She quickly gathered a pile of needles and leaves and spread them on the ground in each shelter. She unfolded one of the Mylar blankets and placed it over the needles. The blankets would tear, but it was better than sleeping directly on the needles. The blanket would also help provide more warmth once everyone got inside.

Everyone crowded into the two shelters. The body heat would have to be enough to keep them warm through the night.

Chase, Jack, Wyatt and Megan crammed into one, while, Evan, Garrett, Greg, Brenda and Bryan squeezed into the other.

It was then Megan realized the group wasn't completely meshed. They still had this natural division between old and new. It wasn't on purpose, but she was still learning to trust the new people. She trusted Chase, Jack and Wyatt with her life. She wasn't quite prepared to rely on the others just yet.

"Did you hear that?" Megan asked in the darkness, as a gunshot echoed.

"Yes," Wyatt replied. "It was just one. Who knows, it could have been McDaniels shooting another one of his men."

That didn't exactly make her feel better, but she accepted the

247

explanation. One less man they had to kill.

Several times throughout the night, they heard gunshots. Megan knew they couldn't be hunting. Either the men were shooting each other or shooting for fun. Neither option was very comforting.

She lay awake most of the night. When she heard the birds start singing, her initial reaction was to stay right where she was. Comfy and safe. She knew it wasn't an option, but for a moment, she allowed herself to appreciate the feeling.

"Wyatt," she whispered, trying not to wake everyone in the shelter.

"I'm awake," he said.

"It's almost dawn."

He yawned. "I know."

He didn't move. Megan began to wonder if he had changed his mind.

She was about to say something when he squeezed her hand, "I need you to know I love you. If things go bad and I tell you to run, you better do it. Do not try to save me or anyone else. You get out of there as fast as you can."

Her breath hitched in her throat at the thought of him dying.

"I will," she said, even though she knew she wouldn't. She

would not leave him to die. Never.

"Megan," he growled, he clearly didn't buy it.

"I will do what I can to save myself," she said again, still refusing to say the word promise.

"You know she won't, Wyatt. Don't waste your breath," Jack said softly.

Megan was instantly on alert. He sounded weak, as if speaking required more energy than he had.

She found her flashlight and shone it on Jack.

She gasped when she saw him.

"Jack!"

"I'm fine. I just need a minute."

"Take your pants off. Let me see your leg," she demanded.

He guffawed, "Brother, do you hear your woman demanding I take off my pants?"

Wyatt didn't laugh, "Do what she says. I want to see as well."

Jack grimaced.

"I'll be okay. It's just a little infected."

"Do it, Jack," Wyatt growled.

Jack shimmied under the sleeping bag for a few minutes.

Megan could see the pain on his face every time he moved.

"There."

Megan shone the light on his thigh. The sight of the injury made her nauseated. A bright red area all the way around the cut was a bad sign. It was swollen. A horrible yellowish ooze was leaking from the area Rosie had left open. Megan covered her mouth and nose when the putrid smell reached her.

Coughing, she took a shallow breath. "Jack, why didn't you say something? This isn't good. I'll get Brenda. She needs to see this."

Wyatt stared at the leg without saying a word.

"She knows," Jack managed to get out. He laid his head back on the pillow, taking deep breaths.

"And what did she say?" Wyatt asked.

"Not much to say. It's infected and not healing like it should."

Wyatt clearly didn't believe him.

"I need some fresh air," Jack said suddenly. He flipped the blanket back over and quickly pulled up his pants.

He didn't take the time to button them before he stumbled out of the shelter. Megan knew the situation was dire when she heard him vomiting.

She thought back to last night and throughout the day. Jack

250

hadn't eaten a thing.

"It's bad, isn't it?" she looked at Wyatt.

His mouth was set in a grim line.

He nodded his head.

Chase sat up. He had been on the other side of Jack.

"He knew this trip would be tough, but he's stubborn. Your mom tried to tell him he needed to rest and let his body heal, but he wouldn't listen. Brenda told him it was badly infected. She used the word 'septic'."

"Why didn't she tell me?" Wyatt half-yelled.

"Jack made her promise not to. They didn't want to worry you."

"You knew?" he looked at Chase with anger and hurt in his eyes.

"I found out yesterday. I accidentally walked in on them bandaging it. They made me promise not to say anything. Willow doesn't know how bad it is," Chase explained. "Jack really wanted to be a part of this. He said he couldn't sit back while his family was at risk."

Wyatt shook his head, "That is about the dumbest thing I have ever heard. He never could do the smart thing."

Evan popped his head in, "We're ready when you are."

251

Megan's stomach dropped and heat flooded her body as she realized it was time to head into war.

"You good?" Evan asked.

She nodded, "Yep, ready to get this over with and get back home to my baby."

They decided to leave the shelters. The extra weight of the tarps would only be a hindrance. If they were successful, they wouldn't need the shelters. If they failed, well, they wouldn't need the blankets.

Jack was leaning against a tree when Megan emerged from the tent. He offered her a wane smile.

She went to him, "You should have told me, Jack. You didn't have to push yourself so hard."

He smiled, "I wasn't going to miss out on this. Besides, I owe somebody for this," he said gesturing to his leg.

"Okay, be careful, please."

"I will. Now, let's get this done."

Everyone headed towards the road that would lead to their victory; or their doom.

Bryan had decided to take on the role of cheerleader. "We can do this guys. Tonight, we will be back at the lodge. Finally, safe."

No one bothered to respond. Each of them was focused on the

task at hand knowing full well his words held no real guarantees. They were walking into a battle that offered very little chance of a roaring success story.

It was David versus Goliath, but the happy ending wasn't a guarantee.

Chapter Twenty-Nine

They spread out in a semi-circle around the massive stone house. With a fine rain falling, it created an eerie mist around the home. Megan took a moment to take it all in. It was a gorgeous home. A curved staircase with high stone walls led to an upstairs deck. Massive wood doors gave the home the look of a real medieval fortress. It was spectacular.

She imagined the home was at least twice, maybe three times as big as the lodge. It sprawled out over the property and the height of the home suggested both floors had high, vaulted ceilings. The dark wood that surrounded the windows and doors created a dramatic look against the stone walls.

This is the kind of home she envisioned some Hollywood celebrity living in. Three sides were surrounded by trees. What was probably once a gorgeous manicured lawn could still be made out in front of the home. The landscaping was beautiful. She was going to hate to destroy it, but if it meant ridding the earth of the vile creatures inside, so be it.

She studied the house and realized it was probably impenetrable as well. Wyatt had said he remembered the supplies were on the bottom floor. Maybe they could set the dynamite on one end and preserve the food that was hopefully still tucked away.

The upstairs deck was one of the many vantage points. Off to the left, there was another smaller deck that would allow a person to see three sides. A similar deck on the opposite side would provide the same vantage point.

"What do you think?" Megan whispered to Wyatt.

"We need to get a little closer to see if anyone is up and about."

He put his hand up in the air and pointed towards the house.

The group advanced, making sure to move slowly and to keep to the trees as much as possible. Once they crossed the tree line in front of the home, they would be completely exposed. That meant they would have to flank the home, leaving the front uncovered.

As they got closer, Megan nearly laughed at what she saw.

Now she knew what the gunshots had been. The men had clearly had a wild night.

"Beer cans?" Evan said in disbelief. "Who has beer? I want a beer."

Megan rolled her eyes. Of course, that's what he chose to focus on.

She blinked a few times. She had thought a shirt was hanging through the rails of the top deck. It was a shirt all right, but the shirt had an arm in it and the arm was attached to a large man passed out on the deck.

"Seriously?" she said under her breath.

"This could be very good for us. I don't see any movement. They're hopefully all still drunk or in too bad a shape to fight back," Wyatt said, sounding a little more upbeat.

"Look," Megan said pointing to several rifles propped up in the corner of the deck.

Chase pulled out a pair of small binoculars to get a better look.

"It's those damn ARs," he said. "They must have an arsenal in there."

Wyatt stood, put his hand in the air again and motioned for everyone to move back.

They retreated back into the forest.

"We need a plan," Wyatt started. "It's obvious that place is easy to defend. I'm guessing there are men ready to take their places at each corner of the house and we know they're armed with semi-automatic weapons. We're only going to have one shot at this."

There were several ideas tossed around about how best to approach but given their small group size and with the sun rising quickly, they needed to decide fast. Ultimately, it was decided to use the dynamite to blow up the arches in the front of the house.

The arches would bring down the top deck and possibly cause more damage to the structural integrity of the house.

If they could just bring the house down on top of the men inside, it would make their battle short and sweet and almost a guaranteed success.

"I'll stay on the front side," Jack said. "If anyone comes out the front, I will take them out."

Megan looked at him, "Jack, the front is completely open. You would be extremely vulnerable."

"I'll set up on the other side of the yard in that thicket. I can use the rifle to pick them off one at a time. They won't see me."

She didn't want to point out the obvious—the men would figure out he was there and spray the area with bullets.

"We have to have that area covered and I am not going to be able to run around much. This is the best place for me," he said in a voice that said he was done arguing.

"Fine," she said not thrilled with the plan, but accepting it for what it was.

Chase, Evan and Garrett volunteered to cover the back of the house.

Wyatt and Megan would be on the right with Greg and Brenda on the left.

"Bryan, you set the dynamite and then join Greg and Brenda," Wyatt instructed.

He looked at Megan, "You sure you are okay with putting the dynamite out?"

Megan's job was to set the dynamite under the arches in front of the double-car garage and then get back to safety. The blast would drop the deck on that side, which would give them an entry point to the home.

She nodded. How hard could it be? Albert had explained how to attach the blasting cap and the fuse could be lit with a lighter or match. Since she was so much smaller, she felt better about lighting a stick of dynamite with Wyatt covering her rather than the other way around.

Everyone voiced their agreement with the plan.

"The fog," Megan gestured around them. "How are we going to see clearly?"

The fog continued to grow and thicken, which could work in their favor but could also make shooting the right people a little tricky.

"Everyone knows their positions. Shoot anyone that comes out of that house. Our main goal is Connor McDaniels. We take him out and we'll create a power vacuum. They'll implode. We don't retreat or call it quits until he is dead," Chase reiterated. "We're close enough that you should be able to see clearly. Before we split up, everyone look at what everyone else is wearing. Remember that before you take a shot."

Brenda was all business, checking her weapon, tucking in her shirt and tightening the laces on her boots. Megan watched her and realized she should probably do the same. The woman was a trained soldier. If she was double checking her laces, Megan was going to, as well.

"Guys, if things look bad, like we don't have a chance of succeeding, get out. Go to the bug-out cabin—not the lodge. Albert radioed earlier, he is taking the kids to the cabin today to be on the safe side," Wyatt said.

"Did something happen?" Megan asked, instantly worried about Caitlin.

"No, he thinks it would be wise, in case some of these guys break away and make a run for the lodge. It's a smart move. They'll be safer there."

Everyone agreed.

"Let's move," Wyatt ordered.

As they approached, Wyatt turned back to Jack who was limping behind. "Keep your eyes on that garage. We may not be able to take them all out if they leave on ATVs. No one escapes."

Jack was out of breath already. "Got it."

Megan fell back to walk with Jack. "Are you sure you are up for this?"

"Yep, I'm okay, Megan. We get through this and then you better believe when we get home I am lying in bed and Willow will be waiting on me hand and foot."

Megan giggled, "Sure she will. She's going to be kicking your butt for not telling her how bad your wound is."

He winked. "She is a lot of fun when she's mad."

Megan touched his arm, "Jack, please be careful. Watch your back. You aren't going to be able to run, so give yourself a head start if we have to get out of there fast."

"We aren't going to be running. We are going to do fine. You have to believe it. Don't be putting any bad juju into the air by being negative."

"Take care of yourself, Jack," she told him before speeding up and falling into step by Wyatt.

Everyone split off to get in position. Bryan carried the dynamite to the edge of the garage and waited to hear the bird call announcing all was clear. They couldn't afford tipping off the men inside. They had one chance. One shot to use surprise to their advantage. Bryan crouched down and crab-walked to the giant stone arches. Megan watched as he laid a stick of dynamite at the base. She was a little sad to destroy such a beautiful piece of architecture, but it had to be done.

She got busy putting her own stick into place and pulling out a lighter—then she heard heavy footsteps above. Someone was coming out on the small deck.

She had two choices, run now or, light the dynamite and then run. If she delayed, the person might see her. If she didn't light the dynamite, the entire plan would be ruined.

With her decision made, she bent down and used her lighter to ignite the fuse on the stick of dynamite. Knowing Wyatt was watching and would shoot the man if she was spotted. She crouched low and rushed back to the hiding spot next to Wyatt.

They watched as the man, threw open the doors to the upstairs room. He was shirtless and smoking a cigarette. The glow of the cigarette was like a beacon in the dawn light, shrouded by the swirling mist. He walked to the edge, scratched himself and then started to urinate over the side. He stumbled to the right and his clumsiness knocked over a semi-full beer can, causing it to dump out over the side onto the stick of dynamite, effectively extinguishing it.

She looked to Wyatt, "Now what?"

"Plan B."

"Plan B? What is Plan B?" she was frantic. They didn't have a second plan. "Wyatt, what are we doing?"

Just then another man opened the side door of the garage on the ground floor. He too looked in rough shape. He was carrying a rifle slung over one shoulder.

"Quit pissing off the porch, man," he said with frustration.

The guy up above chuckled, "Watch where you're walking."

The man below directed the beam of a flashlight to the area where the urine pooled.

"What the?"

"What?" the man above said leaning over the railing.

Megan froze. He had found the dynamite.

Their surprise was blown. Megan started to panic. They wouldn't walk out of here alive if they didn't have the element of surprise.

Wyatt whistled. It was the signal for the attack.

Megan looked towards the front of the house. The dynamite hadn't exploded.

"Take cover," Wyatt said in a low voice.

She saw what at first appeared to be a shooting star, but it was far too close to the ground.

It was a stick of lit dynamite. It was sparking and creating a spectacular display. Before it hit the ground it exploded. The front of the house crumbled in places, but the stone was solid. What would have leveled a typical home barely did any damage to the fortress in front of her.

The sound of the explosion rang in her ears.

The smoke and the mayhem that followed left her stunned. There were men pouring out of the home, firing weapons in every direction.

Wyatt was shooting every few seconds. The sound of the gunshots made the ringing in her ears even worse.

"You good?" Wyatt shouted over the bedlam unfolding below.

She stared at him, watching as he pulled the trigger over and over. She was enthralled with how methodical he was. It mesmerized her; much like a fire dancing did to anyone that allowed themselves to be hypnotized by the flames.

"Megan! Shoot!"

Her vision cleared and everything was blissfully silent. It felt like she was in a bubble. She aimed her rifle and pulled the trigger.

Bullets were spraying the hillside all around the house.

"Watch yourself, Megan!" he shouted sinking into the ground to protect himself from the bullets.

She quickly imitated his actions and hoped the ground would

swallow her up.

Megan couldn't believe she hadn't been shot yet. There were bullets peppering the area where she and Wyatt were hunkered down.

The men were either the worst shots in the world or they were shooting just to shoot. They were firing as if there was no reason to worry about running out of ammunition. That was not a good sign.

While reloading her rifle, she took a second to check on everyone else.

Greg was lying on the ground, exposed. He wasn't moving. Megan prayed he wasn't badly hurt or dead.

The men kept coming out of the house, shooting. It reminded her of an anthill. They just kept coming!

Megan watched as Brenda belly crawled towards Greg. She held her breath as she watched Brenda put two fingers on his neck. When Brenda began to drag the man back to the safety of their original spot, Megan breathed a sigh of relief.

He had to be alive. Brenda wouldn't risk her life to save a dead man, right?

"McDaniels!" Wyatt shouted.

Megan turned to see where Wyatt was looking. The leader of

the horrible men had his leg thrown over the top balcony where the other man had been standing. He was going to jump.

Wyatt aimed, but couldn't get a clear shot.

McDaniels had made it over the balcony and was running into the trees.

"I can't waste the ammo, we're running out," Wyatt said in frustration.

Shooting at a moving target in the trees was pointless.

"We can't let him get away, Wyatt!"

He nodded, picked up the box of ammunition lying on the ground and headed towards the back of the house to get a better shot.

Megan had a moment of panic at the thought of being alone, but quickly tamped it down. She needed to take out as many of the men as possible.

She took a moment to scan the area. There was a small shed off to the side of the home. The sun was breaking the horizon, which made it easier for her to see.

Evan, Chase and Garrett were running towards the shed. Brenda and Bryan were running from their position off to the side of the house.

One of McDaniels' men had spotted the group and opened fire.

Megan screamed when she saw Brenda drop to the ground. The rest made it to the shed. She waited to see if Brenda was going to get back up. She didn't move.

Anger surged through Megan; that man was going to die. She aimed and fired. Down he went.

"Take that, you big jerk," she murmured.

Megan watched Brenda, praying the woman would show some sign of life. Nothing. Her heart dropped at the thought of Brenda dying. She was just starting to get to know her better.

They weren't best friends, but she would miss her. Miss her skills and that dry sense of humor.

She turned to check on Jack.

He was still shooting, taking out the men who were trying to escape out the front doors. It was boom, quiet, boom, quiet. Jack was taking too long to reload, but every shot found its mark. Still their rifles were no match for the semi-automatic weapons the other men had. They were putting out ten times as many bullets making the likelihood of getting hit by a stray bullet that much higher.

Megan loaded her rifle and looked for her next target.

"No!" she yelled to nobody in particular.

Two men were aiming a giant rocket launcher directly at Jack's location. She knew nothing about military weapons, but she knew a rocket launcher when she saw one. The billionaire owner of this house must've been seriously well-equipped.

She quickly took the shot and took out one of the men next to the launcher.

As she reached for another bullet, there was a commotion at the shed. A man was using a torch to ignite small piles of twigs at each corner. She quickly reloaded, ready for her next shot.

The last time she had seen Chase, Evan, Garrett and Bryan, they had gone in there.

Her attention switched back to the man with the launcher.

She took a deep breath, "First Jack and then Chase," she said reaching down to grab another bullet.

Nothing.

"No!" she sat up and quickly felt deep in her pockets for a bullet. There was nothing. She felt around on the ground, hoping one had fallen out of her pocket. Nothing.

Megan gave a strangled cry. Then remembered Wyatt had taken the box with him!

"No, no, no. This can't be happening. Please, God. Just one more bullet. Please!" she wailed. She had one loaded and that was it.

She wasted several precious seconds trying to find a way out of the horrible situation she found herself in.

Jack or the four members of the group trapped in the shed. Her eyes darted back and forth. She could see Jack lying on the ground loading his rifle. His attention was focused on the front doors. He didn't seem to notice the man to the left, aiming a giant machine of death at him.

Her eyes darted to the shed. The man had ignited two fires and was working on a third at the corner of the shed. It would go up in a flash.

She frantically looked around for Wyatt. She needed him. She needed his gun and his guidance. He would know what to do. No, he would have already done it.

Megan closed her eyes, begging for mercy and praying for divine intervention.

Chapter Thirty

"Please don't make me make this decision," she whispered. A tear slipped down her cheek as she thought of her options.

She loved Jack. He had become her best friend next to Wyatt. Wyatt loved Jack. Willow, Rosie and Ryland all flashed through her mind. She couldn't leave them without their brother, husband, son and father.

She thought about the four men trapped in the burning shed. Evan had Tara, but the other men were single. Would their absence be as big a loss as Jack's? They had the remaining explosives too—and with McDaniels holed up, that may be their only way to get at him.

Were four lives more valuable than one? Four lives that were outsiders a couple weeks ago, or someone who she now considered family?

That wasn't her call to make. She knew deep down what to do, but she couldn't.

It was truly gut-wrenching. Her insides felt like they were being twisted into knots as she weighed the importance of each of the men's lives. She didn't want to admit it, but she had grown fond of each of them.

Every one of them held a place in her heart and each of them deserved to live. Who was she to make this decision?

She cursed the fates for putting her in such an impossible situation.

When she opened her eyes, her decision had been made.

She aimed the rifle, paused and then pulled the trigger. It all felt like it was happening in slow motion. The recoil from the rifle threw her shoulder back as the gun bucked. Megan held her breath as she watched her target.

He dropped. The torch fell to the ground. At the same moment the man with the torch fell dead to the ground, there was another explosion.

"Jack!" she screamed.

Megan sobbed as she watched the area where Jack had been, explode in a fiery inferno.

"I'm so sorry, I'm so sorry."

But her attention was soon drawn back to the barn. The two small fires that had been lit were quickly growing. The shed was going up in flames with the group trapped inside.

She had expected to see them run out. When they didn't, she knew they were trapped inside. The man had trapped them and was going to burn them alive.

Megan looked around, trying to find a way to get to the shed without getting shot. The fire burning out of control where Jack had been hit would provide her enough cover. It was the long way around, but she had to try.

Megan raced towards the fire and then behind it. She couldn't stop herself from looking to see if by some miracle Jack had survived. There was a small depression in the ground in the exact spot she had seen him last. There was no possible way he could have survived. With his injury, he couldn't have run away fast enough.

There had been gunshots, but she had no idea if they were aimed at her or someone else. She chose the area where Brenda and Greg had sheltered as her next destination. She made it.

It was then she saw Greg's lifeless body.

"No!" she cried out.

Her mind was trying to process it all. Jack, Greg and Brenda were all dead. She hadn't seen Wyatt in a while.

What if he was lying dead somewhere or shot and needing help?

Yelling brought her back to the task at hand. She realized it was the men inside the shed screaming for help. Megan was not about to let Jack's death be for nothing. She would not let those men die.

Megan raced past Brenda's body lying on the ground, but

didn't stop to check on her. Stopping for even a second could cost more lives.

She reached the shed and quickly found the door. It wouldn't budge.

"Dammit!" she shouted. "Hold on, guys. I'm trying!"

Megan looked around for a rock to hit the lock on the door. She found one and started pounding on the lock.

It wasn't doing any good. The heat from the fire was making it difficult for her to stay close.

She looked back to the man holding the smoldering torch. He didn't have a gun.

Megan scanned the area. Her eyes landed on a shovel lying on the ground a few feet away from the barn.

The fire had engulfed one side of the shed. She grabbed the shovel. Using the head of the shovel like an ax, she continued to hit the wooden door. She thought back to how she'd thrown herself against the lodge door when she'd first found it and eventually broke it down with sheer determination.

Just when she thought her efforts would be futile, the wood cracked. She hit it again, splintering the wood. A few more good whacks and she had made a good size hole.

"Get back," Chase shouted.

She complied and the large man came crashing through the door a few seconds later.

He went right back in, coming back with Bryan, who was nearly carrying Garrett. Evan was right behind them.

They were all coughing. She prayed her efforts weren't too late.

"We're fine," Chase said, before launching into another coughing fit.

"We need to get out of here," Evan said. "Where is everyone else?"

Megan looked at Chase. "Jack's dead."

All four men looked at her with shock and sadness.

"Wyatt?"

She shrugged, "I don't know. He took off after McDaniels."

"Let's move," Chase said, heading towards the back of the house.

Garrett seemed to recover with the fresh air and managed to walk himself.

"There's a barn back here. If McDaniels was running, he would probably head there," Chase said leading the way.

Behind them the fully engulfed shed fire created an orange

glow. Bodies were strewn about the area—but one was walking towards them.

"Behind us!" Megan alerted the group. She was hoping one of them still had some bullets.

"Brenda?" Bryan said in disbelief.

The woman was holding her arm across her stomach. Bryan ran to aid her.

"Where are you hit?" Megan asked. She had seen her drop and had run right by her thinking she was dead. She suddenly felt a twinge of guilt.

"Shoulder. I'll live. Where we headed?" she asked, all business.

"Barn. We need to find Wyatt and see if he took out McDaniels," Chase answered.

The gunfire was sporadic now.

"Are they shooting each other?" Megan asked. "If we're all here, who else," she stopped.

Wyatt. Wyatt was unaccounted for.

"Greg?" Evan asked as he looked around.

Brenda shook her head, "He didn't make it."

Evan looked away, trying desperately to hide his grief.

"That's a lot of gunfire. We better go check it out," Chase said.

"Hard telling if they're aiming or just shooting. They aren't the sharpest tools in the shed," Bryan mumbled. "They came out of the house shooting blindly."

When they reached the barn, they spread out, just in case there was anyone holed up inside.

Megan was given a handful of bullets.

Chase held up three fingers, silently counting down. On three, they burst through the large double doors, guns at the ready.

Megan nearly wept with joy when she saw Wyatt kneeling in front of an elderly man and woman and a little girl.

"You're alive!" she wailed.

His face was grim as he untied the couple and little girl who clung tightly to the older woman.

"Meet Harry and Linda. This is their house. And this little cutie is Emma, their granddaughter," Wyatt informed them as the couple nodded their heads. As soon as the little girl was untied, she hugged her grandmother tight.

"McDaniels?" Chase asked.

"He is hiding in some shack behind here," he replied. "I heard yelling and came to help. I just happened to stumble on these two."

The old man rubbed his hands together, trying to get the circulation moving.

"It's an outhouse," Harry informed them.

"Perfect. Who has the dynamite?" Wyatt asked like he was asking for the remote to a television.

Megan was in awe of his ability to be so calm. He was acting as if he did this on a daily basis. That's when she realized he actually had done this on a daily basis. This was a job he had done on many occasions.

"I have some," Bryan offered.

"Good, let's plant it and blow him off the face of this earth. It seems fitting he will die in a pile of—" Wyatt stopped, looking at the elderly woman in front of him.

"Got it," Bryan said. They all knew what he was going to say.

"I'll cover you," Chase said, following Bryan out the door.

"Stay here," Wyatt ordered Megan and Brenda. "You know what to do if one of them tries to come in."

"Yes, sir," Brenda replied.

Megan turned to the couple. They looked like walking skeletons. Their fragile skin was stretched tight across their bones. There was bruising on their faces and arms. They had been sorely mistreated. It was a miracle they were alive. Emma

276

appeared to be healthier, at least physically but the look of terror on her face told a different story.

"We'll get you out of here," Megan said with a soothing voice.

The old woman was crying.

"Thank you. Bless you all. Bless you," Linda repeated.

Megan couldn't imagine the horrors they had been through as she looked down at the little girl who looked to be Caitlin's age but instead of her daughter's dark straight hair, Emma's was blonde and curly.

Seconds later there was a spurt of gunfire followed by a massive explosion that shook the rafters in the barn. Wyatt, Chase and Evan had, hopefully, found McDaniels.

Brenda looked up, "We need to get out of here. They may have gotten a little carried away with the dynamite."

Just then Wyatt came through the door, "Time to move."

Evan and Chase ran in and each grabbed one of the elderly couple and Megan grabbed the child.

Megan could smell the smoke. Their explosion had started a fire. They didn't need to be dealing with a forest fire. Sparks rained down on them as they ran away from where the explosion had gone off.

The group ran around the back of the house, using it as cover.

Megan felt a few raindrops and hoped it would be enough to extinguish the fires burning all around them.

Her wish was granted. The skies opened and released a downpour of rain.

"In here," the old man said.

He opened a door and they found themselves in the garage.

An ATV was parked towards the front.

"Does that work?" Wyatt asked.

"It has been. These guys have been using it for the past couple months. I heard it running yesterday."

Wyatt looked around. Megan knew the instant he realized Jack wasn't with them.

He looked at her, asking the question.

She looked at her feet, gathered the courage to meet his eyes.

The pain she saw when he got her silent message was nearly more than she could stand.

Chase put a hand on his shoulder. Everyone else looked away.

"Greg?" he asked.

Chase shook his head, delivering yet another blow.

"Later. Let's finish this," Wyatt said with such conviction it snapped everyone to attention.

The rain that had been pounding against the roof and the ground outside came to a sudden halt stopping as fast as it had started.

He looked at the group, before designating Brenda to stay in the garage with the couple and child.

"Guard them. We'll clean up the rest of the garbage out here and then we are getting out of here," Wyatt told her.

The rest of them walked out, hugging the side of the garage wall. There were four men standing in the center of what would have been the yard. They all looked a little shell-shocked.

When they saw Wyatt, they all dropped their weapons and held up their hands.

"We don't want any problems. We were just obeying orders."

Wyatt glared at them, his weapon trained on the one that was talking.

"We can go with you. We can fight for you. We don't have anywhere else to go."

Crack!

The man looked shocked as the bullet pierced his chest. He looked at Wyatt before falling face forward to the ground.

Chase raised his gun when one of the men made a move to

grab the gun he had dropped. Wyatt shot him in the head. The other two men were executed within seconds.

Megan knew this was his way of avenging Jack's death. A week ago, his actions would have shocked and maybe even scared her. In this moment, she wished she had been the one to do it.

"Spread out. If there are any other survivors, kill them. No questions. They are not coming back with us," Wyatt ordered.

They split up. There were a few single gunshots, but when Megan didn't hear a semi-automatic gun, she breathed a sigh of relief.

After nearly an hour of searching around the area, she heard Wyatt whistle. He wanted everyone back at the house. She was relieved she had not come across any of McDaniels' men.

Wyatt had the garage door open.

"We are loading this up," he pointed to the ATV. "Brenda will take Linda and Emma back to the lodge. Harry will walk back with us."

"Load it up?" Bryan asked.

"Food. We take what we can load and try to make a trip back. If not, we'll come back in the spring. Most of it is ours from their little raid."

Everyone got to work, packing as much as they could onto the ATV and the small trailer they found in the garage before filling their packs. Megan didn't want to ever come back.

She helped Harry pack a few things in a backpack. He insisted on carrying something. She worried even a five pound pack would be too much for his emaciated body, but he was a fighter. She knew how a strong will to survive could drive a person to do things they normally wouldn't be able to do.

She herself had experienced it and wasn't about to deny this man that same gratification.

Chapter Thirty-One

The walk back to the lodge was somber. Wyatt had radioed Albert, telling him the coast was clear and he could take the women and children back to the lodge. Albert didn't ask about the outcome or any details. Megan had been listening to the conversation, wondering what Wyatt would say. It was a brief conversation.

They moved much slower than they had on the trip over. Each of them lost in thought. Megan fought back the tears that threatened to flow every time she thought about Jack.

Wyatt had requested Brenda not tell his mom or Willow about Jack. That was something he needed to do in person.

Megan felt the guilt as heavy as the pack on her back. She could have saved him. She was the one who chose to let him die.

Did she dare tell Wyatt what happened?

He would never forgive her, surely.

Megan looked up and stared at the sun burning high and bright in the sky. The fog had burned off and the blast of rain had washed the area clean once again.

There hadn't been a clear day in weeks, but today, it was beautiful. The gloom that clung to her made it impossible for her to appreciate it.

On a normal day, if the sun had been this inviting, she would get the kids together and play a game of baseball. She wasn't sure she or the kids could ever enjoy the game again. It would always bring back memories of the game that had ended in gunfire and Jack being stabbed.

"You okay?"

"What?" Megan realized Wyatt was talking to her.

"Are you okay?"

"Oh, yeah, I don't know, lost in thought I guess."

His expression had been fixed since he learned about Jack. There wasn't anger or sadness. It was just set in a permanent, all-business look.

"You?" she asked, already knowing he would say he was fine.

"Ready to get home. Kind of. I'm not really looking forward to that reunion."

Megan gulped back the giant lump in her throat.

She didn't know what to say. Sorry was inadequate. She should apologize because it was her fault Wyatt's brother was dead.

"Are we close?" she asked instead. It seemed like a safe subject.

"Yeah, probably more than half way."

The sound of an ATV engine made Megan's stomach drop. She reached for her gun. Wyatt put his hand on the barrel as she raised it up.

"It's probably Albert or Brenda coming back to get Harry. I asked her to. He's pretty weak and I don't think he can make it much farther."

"Oh," she said, lowering the gun, feeling her pounding heart return to a normal rhythm.

Brenda appeared up ahead, steering the four-wheeler towards them.

"Harry, you go on back with, Brenda. We'll be there soon enough," Wyatt instructed.

At first, Megan thought the man would argue, but he must have known he didn't have the strength to carry on.

"Thank you. I appreciate all you have done, Wyatt. Your dad would have been proud," he said, crawling behind Brenda on the ATV.

"How's the arm?" Chase asked Brenda.

"Fine. Rosie put some stuff on it and bandaged it up. I told her to hurry so I could get back out here."

Brenda looked at Wyatt, "There were a lot of questions."

He nodded, "That's fine. Let them know we will be there after dusk I imagine."

"Yes, sir. You ready?" she asked the elderly gentleman who was clinging to her waist. His head was resting against her back.

"Ready."

"See you in a bit, Harry," Wyatt called out before Brenda fired up the engine and took off.

Megan didn't want to return to the lodge. How could she possibly face Willow?

Her mind flashed to Ryland. Ryland's dad had been killed. The boy looked up to his father and now, he was going to grow up without a dad.

It was too much. The grief crashed over her catching her off guard. Her knees buckled and before she knew what was happening, she hit the ground.

Wyatt was instantly by her side.

"What happened? Are you hurt?" He frantically searched her body, pulling her jacket open and then searching her back.

She couldn't answer. She shook her head no, but he wasn't getting the message. All she could do was sob. The guilt and grief were too much for her to bear.

When Wyatt found no injuries, he leaned back and looked at her. A look of understanding crossed his face.

"You guys go on ahead. We'll catch up," he told the group who had gathered around.

Chase seemed to understand and commanded the other men to keep moving.

"Let it out, Megan. Let it out," Wyatt soothed, rubbing her back.

Megan wanted to tell him to go away, but she couldn't form the words.

"I'm sorry," she managed to gurgle out. "I'm so sorry, Wyatt."

"Megan, you can't be sorry. It isn't your fault. The man responsible is dead. There is nothing more we can do."

She vehemently shook her head, "No! You don't understand. It was me. I did it!"

"What? You did what, Megan?"

"Jack!" she wailed. "It's my fault."

"Megan, it isn't your fault. Jack knew exactly what he was getting into. We all did. It could have been any one of us."

Megan cried harder. She had to tell him. There was no way she could live with the weight of the guilt. There was a good chance she would be leaving them once he found out she had chosen to save the others instead of his brother.

A sudden calm washed over her as the resolve to clear the air took hold. She refused to live with the guilt.

Taking a deep breath, Megan stared Wyatt right in the eye, "You don't understand. I could have saved him. I chose not to."

Wyatt leaned back on his heels. He didn't say anything. She knew he was waiting for an explanation.

"Bryan, Chase, Evan and Garrett were all trapped in the shed. A man had a torch and was lighting it on fire. I knew I had to take him out."

Wyatt nodded.

"There were two other men with some RPG type thing. They were aiming it directly at Jack. Jack was kicking some serious butt and took out quite a few of the men. I shot one of the men, but the other one kept going."

A grim look crossed Wyatt's face.

"You shot the man with the torch."

She fought back the tears that threatened to start pouring out again.

"Yes. I only had one bullet, Wyatt," she whispered. "I had one bullet and an impossible decision."

Wyatt didn't say anything for several long minutes.

"Okay," he said, standing up and brushing his pants off.

"Wyatt. I am so sorry. I didn't know what to do. I thought of the four men burning alive. I couldn't let it happen."

He turned to look at her, still kneeling on the ground.

"You did what you had to do. It was for the good of the group as a whole. You chose to save four lives instead of one."

His voice was cold, but not mean. It was a commander talking to his soldier, not a man talking to the woman he loved.

Megan instantly regretted unburdening herself. She should have never told him. Now she made her grief and guilt his. He had enough to deal with and she made it worse.

If she thought the guilt was bad before, it was nearly unbearable, now.

They started walking again, with Wyatt ahead of her. They didn't speak. She wondered if he would ever talk to her again.

Her mind started to whir as she thought of her future. She was going to have to leave the lodge. She would not make them look at her, the woman who killed the man they loved. Could she stay through winter?

She would have to try. She couldn't risk taking Caitlin into a snowy winter simply because people were going to treat her with malice. She would have to stay strong and deal with the hate that was sure to come her way.

Another thought popped into her head.

What if they kicked her out?

A strangled cry escaped her throat as she thought of being kicked out with nowhere to go. Would they do such a thing?

Wyatt loved her, but he loved his brother, too. Willow, Rosie and Ryland would encourage him to push her out.

Wyatt had stopped walking and stood in front of her.

"Megan, I think it's best if we keep what happened before Jack's death between us. Okay?"

"Are you sure? I don't want to lie to them. They deserve to know what happened."

"It isn't lying. They don't need to know. It doesn't change the outcome. It would cause problems for the whole lodge."

She understood what he was saying. Deep down, she was relieved no one else would have to know what she did.

"Megan?"

She didn't want to look at him.

"Megan?"

"What?"

"Look at me."

She took a deep breath, preparing herself for his anger and hurt.

"You did the right thing. You saved the lives of four men. The explosives they had were imperative to killing McDaniels. You have to know that. You made a decision based on the needs of many over the needs of one."

She nodded, unable to speak. His voice was soft. Her boyfriend had returned. He was saying the words to reassure her and comfort her.

He looked thoughtful, "Jack was in bad shape. I don't know that he would have made it back to the lodge and I think he knew that, which was why he insisted on coming. The position he chose to take was the most obvious. He knew it wasn't a good tactical move, but it provided him with the best advantage. He was an intricate part of our success. His death has meaning. He died saving the people he loved."

The tears could not be held back. They flowed freely down her face, soaking her neck and the high collar of her shirt.

He hugged her holding her tight. She wrapped her arms around his chest and listened to the gentle thud of his heart. They stood that way for a long time. She felt dampness on her shoulder and knew he too was releasing the pain.

He took a deep breath and stepped back, quickly wiping his

eyes.

"We better get moving."

He grabbed her hand, squeezed it and started moving.

Megan wanted to cry with relief and hurt at the same time. He wasn't angry. He didn't blame her. Her secret was safe. She could stay at the lodge.

When they got closer, Megan stopped walking. The rest of the men had waited. No one wanted to be the one to reveal what had happened.

Greg and Jack's death were going to be incredibly hard for them all to accept. Jack's death would be especially difficult.

"We better get this over with," Wyatt said moving forward to cross the stream.

"They're gonna know," Chase said. "They're gonna know the moment we walk through those doors."

"There is no way to soften the blow. Be ready to catch Willow or my mom. I have no idea how hard this will hit them."

Wyatt turned to Megan, "Can you take care of Ryland? He seems close to you."

"Of course. I will do whatever I can to make this easier."

Once again, guilt slammed into her. She was going to have to comfort the boy who lost his dad because she chose not to save him.

Chapter Thirty-Two

Each of them walked single file through the door. Megan walked in front of Wyatt. Rosie was rubbing an ointment on Linda's wrists and she looked up when she saw the procession.

Willow stopped what she was doing at the stove and watched as well.

No one said a word. He didn't think anyone even took a breath. The saying "you could hear a pin drop" wasn't even close to describing the silence in the room.

Wyatt met his mother's eyes before quickly looking away and shutting the door.

"No!" Willow cried. "No! Wyatt! No! Where is he?"

Wyatt walked to her and wrapped his arms around her. She burst into sobs, hunching forward, unable to stand.

Rosie quickly put one hand on the table for support. Linda reached out and grabbed her free hand, offering her sympathy without saying the words.

Chase walked to stand next to Rosie. Wyatt knew he was ready to catch her should she collapse.

Caitlin popped her head over the upstairs railing. "They're back!" she said running down the stairs.

She bounded down the stairs in typical childlike innocence, unaware of the dark cloud hanging in the room.

The little girl rushed to her mom and Megan squeezed her daughter, holding Wyatt's gaze.

He hoped she could shake off the guilt she was feeling. There was nothing she could have done differently to make the situation any better.

They all knew death was a real possibility when they went on their march to war. He knew Jack had accepted the possible outcome. He knew without a doubt his brother never would have been okay if Megan had chosen to save him and let the others die.

"Where's dad?" Ryland asked, looking around the room.

His eyes settled on Wyatt holding his mother.

"Mom?"

Wyatt didn't know what to say. He couldn't say the words, couldn't get them out.

It was Bryan who surprised him.

"Your dad is a hero, Ryland." He walked over and extended his hand, "I want to shake hands with the son of the man who saved all our lives."

Ryland put his hand out, still not fully grasping the situation.

He looked to Megan, "He…died?"

Wyatt watched as Megan fought back the tears. She peeled Caitlin off her and walked to Ryland, dropping down to get eye to eye with him.

"He did, honey. I am so very sorry. He was so proud of you. He fought so hard. It is like Bryan said. He saved all our lives. He is a hero."

Albert had been sitting quietly at the table, "Greg?"

Chase shook his head.

"Dammit," Albert muttered.

"You killed them all?" Rosie asked in a steady voice.

Wyatt looked her in the eyes, "Every last one."

She took a deep breath, schooled her features and walked to Wyatt.

"Willow, dear, let's go upstairs," she said softly.

Willow was uncontrollably crying.

Everyone in the room looked away. Her pain and suffering was palpable and it cut through each of them.

Ryland appeared to be in shock. Once Rosie had Willow safely up the stairs, Wyatt went to him.

"You want to talk about anything?" he asked the young boy who had yet to say anything else.

"How did he die?"

Wyatt looked to Megan for help. Should he tell him? Was he too young?

Megan grabbed Ryland's hand and led him to the table. She gestured for Wyatt to sit across from him.

Harry extended his frail arm and placed it on Ryland's back, "Your dad was a Godsend, young man. He saved me, my dear wife, and our little Emma. I didn't get the chance to meet him, but I know he sacrificed himself to make sure all of us would be okay."

Linda, who looked to be in bad shape, had tears streaming down her cheeks.

"I'm so sorry, Ryland," she said in a weak voice. "I'm so sorry, but I too am so thankful I got the chance to meet you and your mom."

Ryland turned back to Wyatt, "How did he die, Uncle Wyatt? Please, tell me!"

Wyatt took a deep breath, "To be honest, I don't know for sure. There were a lot of men. Your dad held a position that allowed him to kill them as they came out of the house. I don't know how many men your dad killed, but you can imagine that they got a little angry."

Ryland grinned, completely taking Wyatt off guard.

"I hope he killed a whole bunch of them."

Megan stood next to Ryland, "He did. He absolutely did."

Wyatt was relieved when Ryland didn't press for details about Jack's death. The young boy didn't need to know all the graphic details.

"Are we going to have funerals for my dad and Greg?" he asked.

"Yes. We will. I think we need to give your mom some time and then we will plan a funeral," Wyatt explained.

Ryland was quiet for a few minutes before he stood.

"I better go check on my mom. I'm the man of the family now and dad always told me I had to take care of her if something ever happened."

"Yes, you do. If you need any help, you let one of us know. You don't have to do it all on your own. We are all in this together. We will all help you and your mom," Wyatt assured him.

"Okay. Thank you. Come on Duke, we gotta go check on mom."

The dog jumped up and followed him up the stairs.

Wyatt excused himself from the group and went into the bathroom to clean up. He heard a knock on the door.

"Thought you may want some hot water," Megan said holding out the steaming tea kettle.

"Actually, yes, that would be great. Here," he said handing her one of the clean towels. "I know you want to clean the grime off, as well."

She took the towel and closed the door behind her.

Wyatt poured the hot water into the bowl before adding some of the water from the jug that was always left in the bathroom for quick cleanups.

Megan sat on the edge of the tub, staring down at her feet. "It feels very weird."

"Yes, it does and it will for some time. We'll have to adjust to a new normal all over again."

She stood, dipped her towel in the water and sat back down on the tub edge. "I'm tired of constantly adjusting. Just when you think things are going to be okay for a bit, surprise, a crazy mad man wants to kill you." She smiled. "Not once, but twice. How does this happen to the same group of good people twice in the space of a year? We must have some really bad karma floating out there."

Wyatt shrugged, "It's life. I imagine in a few weeks or months, there will be a new threat. It is never going to end. We are always going to be fighting against bad guys, Mother Nature and probably wild animals eventually. This life is going to be anything but boring."

Megan sighed and finished wiping down her face, neck and arms.

"I'm beat. I'm going to read with Caitlin and then I think I will crash."

"Aren't you going to eat?" he asked.

"I'm not hungry."

He looked thoughtful for a second, "I don't think anyone is. I better go put away whatever it was Willow was making before we came in and destroyed her world."

Megan winced. "Harsh."

"Sorry. I'm not saying you, I am saying we. As in all of us, including Jack. He knew what he was doing."

"I know, I know," she said, grabbing his neck and giving him a quick kiss. "See you in a bit."

Wyatt spent a couple more minutes alone in the bathroom. He took a few deep breaths and fought back the emotion that came bubbling to the surface.

The lodge did feel weird without Jack. Greg had made his mark as well. It was going to be hard to create a new normal. A wave of grief crashed over him like a tidal wave. Jack had been his best friend. He was the guy who understood him. He always lightened up the mood. He was so easy going. Wyatt had always been the serious one.

Wyatt splashed water on his face, demanding he pull himself together.

"I'm good," he whispered to the reflection in the mirror. "I'm good."

Wyatt opened the door to find Chase, Evan and Bryan sitting at the table. They each had a bowl of something, but none of them were eating.

"What's up?" he asked. Bryan looked up from the bowl, "Your mom came down and said we better eat. She said Willow made a good stew to warm our bellies after our journey and we better eat it."

Wyatt had to smile.

He knew they weren't all that hungry, but when Rosie said to do something, even the biggest, burliest man did it.

"Where are Harry, Linda and Emma?"

Chase blew on a bite of stew, "Albert is getting them settled in his room tonight."

"You better get a bowl of stew before your mom comes back," Evan said, completely serious.

Wyatt didn't want to eat, but he didn't want to hurt Willow further.

"Fine."

He scooped up some of the stew. He inhaled the steam and was pleasantly surprised by the aroma.

"It is really good," Bryan said.

"Garrett?" Wyatt asked.

Chase had a strange look.

"He's only nineteen. All of this has overwhelmed him. He headed out to the tent to chill for a while," Chase explained.

Wyatt understood the kid's need to get away from it all. It was a lot to take in. Wyatt had learned a long time ago not to stop and think about all the death. If Garrett allowed himself to see the faces of all of the men that died today, it would eat him alive.

"I'll talk to him," Chase said, reading Wyatt's mind.

"Good. We don't need him getting all crazy and caught up in his head. We still have a lot of work to do."

Bryan looked relieved to be talking about something else.

"Let's make a plan," he said with enthusiasm.

Wyatt realized he was actually glad to plan for the future as well. He needed to stay busy. They all did. If they sat around thinking about the missing members, it wouldn't do anyone any good.

"We need to finish the longhouse. How close to being done is it?" he asked.

"Need to finish the roof, fill the chinks, and hang the door. Jack says," Chase stopped himself. "Said we need to make a fireplace inside. He started making a frame for it. I'm not really sure how to do that."

Albert came into the room, "I'll see if I can find anything in those history books upstairs. We need to get that thing finished. Jack had one he was using for reference. Looks like I'll be joining you boys out there and I want to make sure I stay warm."

Wyatt knew Albert had given up his room to the older couple and their granddaughter. He wasn't sure how long they would stay, but he wasn't about to kick them out. They would work that out later.

"We can send Garrett out hunting. We really need to restore our food supply," Bryan added.

"Good. It will give him something to focus on, as well. Maybe Ryland will want to go with him," Evan added.

Wyatt had been tossing around an idea, but wasn't sure if he wanted to say it or if anyone wanted to hear it.

"There is still quite a load of supplies back at Harry and

Linda's house. There is enough to get us through the winter."

No one said anything.

He knew it would be difficult to revisit the area. The scene would be horrific in the light of day. He wasn't exactly thrilled about going, but the supplies were a necessity.

"We don't have the time or the luxury to be dramatic. We need food. The food is there. Shoot, a lot of it is ours. The stuff we managed to bring back is nothing. We need more."

Evan cleared his throat, "I'll go."

Wyatt knew Evan's reason for volunteering. They would be able to give Greg a proper burial. Transporting the body back to the lodge wasn't an option and Jack's body had been burned in the explosion.

"Good, you and I will go. We will make a larger sled to pull behind the ATV. We can get there and back in half a day. I don't want to leave a trail right back here so we will need to stop periodically to cover our tracks."

They finished eating their stew in silence.

Brenda appeared seemingly out of nowhere.

She looked at Wyatt, "Can I talk to you?"

He nodded. "Here?"

She shook her head, gesturing to the far corner of the room

near the barricaded front door.

"What's up?" he asked. He had no idea what to expect from her. She was still a bit of a mystery.

Brenda looked uncomfortable.

"I shouldn't be telling you this, but I think it is important you know. Maybe let Megan know, as well."

"What is it, Brenda? Did something happen?"

"No, I wouldn't normally talk about a patient, but, well, in this case it's different. Jack was extremely ill."

Wyatt sighed. "I know that."

She met his eyes, "Wyatt, he wouldn't have survived. Period. I strongly suspect he had sepsis. Even if he had been in a hospital, the chances of him surviving were very slim. Without antibiotics, there was nothing we could have done. Actually, even with antibiotics it still could have gone bad."

Wyatt realized then, she knew about Megan's choice to save the group. Megan had told him about Brenda being shot and laying in the yard. She would have had a clear vantage point of the whole scene.

Brenda was a bit of an odd duck. She never showed any emotion. She had this wall around her that made it impossible to tell what she was thinking or feeling, but in this moment, Wyatt could see how much she cared for Megan.

"Thank you. I will tell Megan."

Brenda looked like she had just relieved herself of a terrible burden.

"Brenda, did Jack know?"

She looked uncomfortable, "Yes. I told him the risks. He knew there was a good chance he would die here. He made me promise to keep my suspicions to myself."

Wyatt knew she was telling the truth. It was a Jack thing to do. He suspected something was up, but hearing it confirmed gave him some peace. Jack died on his own terms.

His brother was still gone and there would still be a great deal of grief, but they would get through this.

With tomorrow's chores planned, Wyatt felt a little better. There was a purpose. They were going to keep moving forward, despite the massive setback. It was what Jack would have wanted.

What he demanded.

Chapter Thirty-Three

Megan was surprised she didn't feel more anxious about Wyatt's trip back to the place where everything had gone so terribly wrong. Deep down she knew Wyatt would be safe.

They had taken several of the semi-automatic weapons, AR-15s, from McDaniels' men and would be taking those along in case they encountered any men who may have escaped. He was armed to the teeth. Last night, he had told her he hoped he saw some stragglers. He wanted to shoot them.

Right now, her attention was focused on Chase, Bryan and Garrett. They were building an actual fireplace under the strict supervision of Albert.

The man was holding a paper and giving directions. They stacked large rocks to form an open box approximately two feet by two feet. Megan watched as Chase covered the rocks with thick mud that had a bit of a reddish tint. She recognized it as the soil, rich in clay, found near the stream.

"You need a lot more clay on there, Chase, or you're gonna burn the place down!" Albert growled. "You have to have a good six inches on the inside. The outside of the firebox needs to be covered as well. Those rocks will crack if they aren't covered."

Megan stared at the structure that was beginning to resemble a fireplace. She was impressed. She could see the rocks stacked on top of one another with a wood frame supporting it.

"You want to hand me that bucket," Chase asked. "The drill sergeant has spoken."

Megan laughed. "But it looks good."

Garrett was on a ladder, adding logs in a similar fashion to how the log cabin was built. The logs were getting shorter the higher the chimney went, resulting in it getting narrower as it went up.

"Megan, can you put those cut logs in that bucket and I will pull it up," Garrett called down to her.

"Sure," she said, locating the short logs that had been scraped of bark. Her mind flashed back to Jack showing them how to hew logs. These were left in their original round shape.

Garrett pulled the rope, lifting the bucket to his spot at the top of the ladder.

"You need more mud on those, Garrett," Albert commanded.

"I know, but I need to get them on first," the frustration in his voice apparent. Bryan was mixing mud made from the clay, water, and soil from the garden area.

"Here, I have another bucket ready," he said, removing the rope from the now empty wood bucket and tying it to the mud bucket.

"How long until it is dry?" Megan asked the man in charge.

"A few days. We will give it a test run. The heat from the fire will help harden the mud," Albert replied, looking down at his notes.

"What is that?" she said gesturing to his paper.

He held it up and showed her. She saw a diagram with notes and instantly recognized Jack's handwriting.

"Oh," she said.

He nodded, "Yep. He had a good plan. I found the book he was using and figured out the rest. We still need to go around the whole cabin and fill in the cracks with the mud. He had already written down the recipe. Once we finish this fireplace, we will get started on the rest of the chinking."

"Okay, well I will leave you guys to it. Let me know when it's ready for the first fire. I will be standing by with a bucket of water," she chuckled.

"Go away, Megan," Chase grumbled. "When it works, don't think you get to sleep out here where it will be toasty warm. You get to sleep in that big, drafty lodge."

She laughed and walked away. She had her own chores to do.

Megan finished plunging the load of laundry and drained the water. Caitlin and Frankie were helping her. Tara was cleaning up inside with Amy helping her.

Willow and Rosie were asked to take the day off. Rosie had protested, but it was evident Willow needed her. The woman had made herself physically ill and Rosie was doing what she could to keep her hydrated. Ryland, who had declared himself his mother's protector, was sticking close by her side, as well.

Linda was very frail and although she had tried to get out of bed, Megan sent her right back in. It was nothing short of a miracle the woman had survived at all. While Emma didn't appear to have any lasting physical problems, she was clearly traumatized. She had yet to say anything to anyone even when the children tried. Instead, she ran into the bedroom with her grandmother. Megan hoped, in time, she would come out of her shell.

"Caitlin, can you and Frankie carry that bucket and I will carry this one," she said lugging the heavy load of wet clothes into the lodge.

Megan left the kids to hang the laundry. Caitlin was telling Frankie all about the hunting trip that brought Brenda to them.

Megan smiled as Caitlin embellished parts of the story and Frankie's eyes widened with shock.

"When you are finished there, I need you two to check the goats and get them fresh water," Megan said, interrupting

Caitlin's story.

Rosie appeared at the top of the stairs.

Megan's heart hurt when she saw the woman's ashen face. She didn't look well either.

"Rosie, are you okay?" she asked, quickly climbing the stairs.

The woman nodded, but it was clear she wasn't okay.

"Just a little tired," she said in a voice so quiet Megan could barely hear.

"You need to rest. You have been up all night. I'll take care of Willow, take a nap."

"I'll be okay. I was coming to get some water."

Megan gently put her arms around Rosie and steered her to her room, "I'll get it. Go lay down for a while. You have a lot on your plate. Please let me take care of you for once."

Rosie didn't try to argue. When they got to the edge of the large bed, Rosie collapsed.

Megan helped her get settled before pulling the blanket over her.

"I'll bring you some water as well. Do you want anything else? Have you had a chance to eat anything?"

Rosie's eyes were closed. "I need to close my eyes for a

minute," she whispered.

Megan fought back the panic. They couldn't lose Rosie. It would kill Wyatt and it would be a blow they couldn't recover from.

She quietly walked out of the room, shut the door behind her and headed across the living space to check on Willow.

Megan opened the door. In the middle of the bed, Willow was curled up in a ball, sobbing. Ryland was sitting beside her, rubbing her back and shoulders, telling her it would be okay.

"Can I get you anything?" she asked. "Your grandma needed to lay down for a bit. I'll be downstairs. Ryland, if you or your mom needs something, just holler, okay?"

He nodded, keeping his attention on Willow.

Megan decided she had better stick close by. Both Willow and Rosie had endured a horrible loss and Megan prayed they would recover.

"I am going to work on sewing some of those old shirts we aren't using, and whatever else I can find, together for the door cover in the longhouse," she informed Tara.

Tara looked at her knowingly.

"She is going to need some time."

"Willow?"

"Yes, Willow but also Rosie. She lost a child. I know she is a strong woman, but she has to give herself time to grieve."

Megan knew Tara was speaking from experience. The woman was still very melancholy and Megan often saw her staring off into space. She seemed to be going through the motions, but never present.

"Maybe you can talk with her. You, unlike anyone else here, has a better understanding," she paused. "It would be good for you, as well, to talk with another person who understands your grief."

Tara gave a small smile, "I don't think anyone understands it. It just is."

"When you're ready. Rosie is sleeping now, but I think she would really appreciate talking with you."

Tara nodded, "I'll check back."

Megan gathered the old shirts and other clothing they had been saving. They were hoping the heavy clothing would help block the cold air that would come through the windows upstairs. Now, they needed a heavy curtain to trap the heat in the longhouse, as well.

They all knew there was a good chance the longhouse would be too cold for anyone to sleep in, even with a fireplace. It wasn't like they had rolls of insulation. They were counting on the mud chinking between each of the logs to be enough to keep the drafts out. If the pioneers managed to survive the cold winters, they could too. It was going to be a trial run and if it proved to be too much, they were going to be sleeping on top of each other in the lodge.

Megan sat in the quiet home, sewing together the torn jeans and shirts that were beyond repair. She could hear Willow cry out on occasion, but didn't disturb her.

"They're back!" Caitlin's voice cut through the quiet of the lodge.

Megan rolled her eyes. So much for Rosie getting some rest.

She put down her work and headed downstairs, shushing Caitlin on the way down.

"Rosie is taking a nap," she scolded. "Linda and Emma are also resting."

"Sorry," the little girl whispered.

Megan walked outside with Caitlin and breathed a sigh of relief when she saw Wyatt get off the ATV. He was in one piece and she didn't see blood. That was always a good sign.

"How is everything?" he asked, the concern obvious on his face.

"Fine. We'll talk later," she said not wanting to say too much in front of the kids.

"Frankie, I'm going to need you to help me unload this," Wyatt said with exaggerated authority making the job sound extremely important.

The boy puffed up with pride. Megan smiled at the way Wyatt directed the boy with a firm, but gentle touch. Wyatt would be a good father figure for Ryland.

Harry came over to look at the supplies loaded on the makeshift sled.

Megan instantly felt horrible. They were looting his stuff.

"Good, you got a lot of it. I don't know how much they got into, but those men were savages. They tore through everything. All my damn scotch, too."

Megan laughed.

Harry winked, "But not all of it. I can go back on your next trip and show you where the good stuff is hidden."

"There's more?" Wyatt said with surprise.

"Well, not a lot of food, but Linda demanded we hide her chocolate and wine and I hid my scotch."

Wyatt laughed.

"Heck yeah, you can go. I would love a nice glass of scotch and I know a few ladies who would love to kick back with a glass of wine."

Harry was looking over the supplies.

"Are you sure you are okay with this," Wyatt asked, clearly feeling guilty himself.

"If you are going to allow us to stay here through winter and the foreseeable future, it is only right. Besides, a lot of this stuff isn't what we had stored anyway. You saved our lives, this is the only way we can repay you," he said getting a little choked up.

Wyatt put his hand out and Harry shook it. "Deal."

"Let me help this strapping young man get all this stuff put away. You two go talk," he said shooing Wyatt and Megan away.

Evan directed Frankie on which bags to take while he took the heavy stuff.

Wyatt and Megan walked to her favorite place under the birch trees.

"How is she?" he asked.

"Willow? The same. Ryland is with her. It's your mom I'm worried about."

"Why? What happened?"

Megan put her hand on his thigh, "Nothing. She's fine, but I think she wore herself out staying up with Willow all night. She hasn't taken any time for herself. She suffered a loss as well."

Wyatt stared up at the trees.

"I know. I don't know what to say to her. First, my sister. Then I leave them alone and my dad is killed. And now, Jack."

"Wyatt, don't you dare put this on yourself. You know you had nothing to do with any of those incidents. I think she needs you now. Talk to her. You two are all you have left. Lean on each other."

He exhaled a long, slow breath.

"I will. I'll go check on her. She'll be okay, Megan. My mom is so strong. After my dad, well, I thought she would be destroyed. She was sad, but she didn't let it consume her. I think we need to keep her busy. She is the type of woman who needs to have her hands doing something, taking care of all of us."

"What about Willow?" Megan asked.

"I think their combined grief is going to hurt them. Let's have my mom help with Linda and Emma while you or Tara takes over the care of Willow. Give them some breathing room. My mom will dote on the newcomers, which is what she does best."

"That is a very good plan. I knew you would have all the answers," she smiled at him.

"Don't try to butter me up, woman."

She laughed.

"We better get back and make sure those kids didn't find any treats. They'll be sharing with the goats," Megan said standing and holding out her hand for Wyatt to take.

They walked back to the lodge, hand in hand. Megan felt better than she had in days. Things felt like they were settling into place, once again. She prayed they would make it through the winter without any further loss. They all needed a break. More than that, they needed hope. Hope for a brighter future.

Epilogue

It had been a long two weeks since they returned to the lodge without Jack and Greg. The time had been filled with a lot of tears, but Megan was relieved to feel like they were coming out on the other side.

Wyatt and Harry had made one last supply run, which filled the pantry and guaranteed they would have plenty of supplies to make it through winter comfortably.

Willow was doing much better. Megan had spent the past ten days by her side, talking, laughing and crying together. She had never allowed herself to be so open with another woman, but Willow needed her and Megan knew she needed Willow just as much.

"You ready?" Megan asked Willow who was stirring a bowl in the kitchen.

Her face lit up, "I am."

"How about you, Rosie?" Willow asked.

She pulled the cover off the surprise they were planning for the evening meal.

"Oh my gosh, I am salivating!" Tara exclaimed when she saw what was under the large lid.

"That looks amazing," Linda said from her perch on one of the stools at the bar with Emma at her side. She was swirling her glass of wine, taking small whiffs every few seconds.

The women had kicked everyone out of the lodge a couple hours ago. They had asked Brenda to stay, but the poor woman looked like she was going to panic. She was not one to hang out in the kitchen. She preferred to be on patrol or cleaning guns.

"The kids are going to lose their minds," Willow said. "Don't you think so Emma?" she asked the little girl who instead of responding ducked her head behind Linda.

Megan picked up her glass of wine, "With the amount of alcohol Harry and Wyatt brought back, we may all lose our minds. At least it isn't Albert's moonshine."

"Hear, hear," Willow chimed in.

They all giggled at once.

"I think it will be the potato toppings that do it. I have never had freeze-dried sour cream. It is pretty close to what I remember sour cream tasting like," Willow said, dipping her finger in the dish.

"Thank you again for sharing with us, Linda," Megan said, gesturing to the feast spread out before them.

"It is nothing, really. I am so glad we have someone to share it with. When my husband bought all this stuff years ago, I thought he had lost his mind. He was ordering cases and cases of all this crazy stuff. We filled an entire room downstairs. I demanded he add some wine to the list. But I think he got a little carried away," she laughed.

"Well, his getting carried away has worked out quite well for us," Tara laughed.

Linda sighed, "I wish those horrible men wouldn't have used so much of it. They were so wasteful. So awful in general." Emma's arms had crept around her and she hugged her granddaughter to her.

The room grew silent.

"Sorry," she said, suddenly realizing talk of the men that had held her captive for months brought Jack's death front and center.

"It's okay," Willow assured her. "We can talk about him. All of them. None of them should be forgotten."

Tara nodded, her own loss still a fresh wound on her heart.

"Let's set the table. Linda, would you light the candles, please?" Megan asked.

She was truly enjoying herself. It was fun to hang out with the girls. She wasn't worried any of them were going to stab her in the back or gossip about what she was wearing or how her hair looked.

These ladies were her true friends. She felt very fortunate to have met them.

Once everything was perfect, Tara was asked to do the honors of inviting everyone in.

It would be their first big group meal together since the loss. Harry, Linda and Emma were officially a part of the group. This was to be a celebration of life in general.

Everyone filed in the back door. There was a lot of excitement as they all got a glimpse of the table that was set up. There were baked potatoes, venison steaks, corn, and a rice dish set out on the bar. Wine glasses were at each place setting.

The surprise was at the end of the bar, carefully covered to hide what was underneath.

"What is it, mom?" Caitlin asked; and not for the first time.

"You have to wait until after dinner."

"Have a seat, everyone," Rosie instructed. "We will be your servers this evening," she said with a twinkle in her eye.

They all managed to squeeze in around the table. The five women remained standing so they could serve the meal.

Willow picked up a bowl that was stacked high with baked potatoes wrapped in foil. She put one on each person's plate.

Megan delivered her tray filled with small bowls.

"What's that?" Ryland asked.

Megan smiled, "This is sour cream, butter, fresh chives and bacon bits to put on your baked potato."

Albert let out a whistle, "I haven't had a loaded baked potato in forever!"

Willow went back to the counter and distributed slices of bread, slathered with butter.

Rosie dished out the corn, while Tara followed behind pouring red wine into each of the adult's wine glass.

"We have something for you guys too," she said to Frankie who looked a little bummed to have an empty glass.

Megan grabbed the bottle of apple cider Linda said she had been saving for when her grandkids came to visit. They never had the chance to drink it before the Raiders arrived.

"Wait," she said to Caitlin who was about to take a drink. "We are going to have a toast."

Linda quickly served the venison steaks that had been resting on the stove.

"This looks absolutely amazing," Wyatt said, making eye contact with each of the women. "You absolutely outdid yourselves."

There was a chorus of 'thank yous'.

"Wyatt," Megan started, "Would you make the toast please?"

He stood, holding his glass of wine.

"Here's to a fresh start. We will never forget those who gave their lives so we could all be here today. Their sacrifice can never be forgotten. We honor them by moving forward."

The moment was honored with a moment of silence following the heartfelt tribute before Wyatt shouted, "Let's eat!"

The dinner was lively with everyone asking for seconds. They talked about Jack and although there were some tears, there was a lot more laughter. They shared stories about Greg and Sandra as well. Sandra had acted as the camp grandmother. She was also baking, reading stories to the kids, and provided a shoulder for anyone to lean on.

Bryan spoke fondly of Greg and how helpful he had been in the beginning. Greg had been one of the men who helped push out Kyle's men. He was not a man to be pushed around. He was stern, but had a real soft spot for the kids. They had relied on Greg a great deal because of his knowledge of off-grid living.

Once everyone declared they couldn't eat another bite and the surprise had all but been forgotten, Willow stood, carried the tray to the cleared table and removed the lid.

"Mom! It's chocolate!" Caitlin screamed.

Everyone started talking excitedly all at once.

"Linda has been so generous to share her chocolate stash with us," Rosie announced. "You are all about to go into a chocolate coma. We have some powdered milk to help wash it down, too!

"What kind of cake is it?" Ryland asked.

Willow smiled, knowing she was about to make his day, "It is chocolate cake, with chocolate filling and chocolate frosting."

Brenda groaned, "I am thinking about kissing you, Linda."

Everyone laughed. Brenda was not the type to joke and her dry tone made it even funnier.

"Kids, I'll make you a glass of milk and adults, you can have milk or wine," Tara announced.

Duke barked, not wanting to be left out of the festivities. Megan cut off a few chunks of the venison, cut up a baked potato and served the ecstatic dog. He scarfed it down and instantly and started to look for more.

The cake was polished off without even a crumb leftover.

"How about a game of Bridge for the adults and the kids can play that Life game they have had their eye on?" Rosie said.

"How about a nightcap to go with it," Harry said, holding up a bottle of his favorite scotch.

There were more cheers as most of the kids raced upstairs but Emma remained behind holding Linda's hand. Brenda and the men cleared the table and quickly washed the dishes while Rosie and Tara set up the Bridge game.

Megan and Willow had gone outside together to walk to the outhouse.

"You doing okay?" Megan asked her on their way back.

Willow stopped, inhaled deeply and stared up at the stars.

"I am. I will always miss him, but he would not want me to be miserable. I'm still sad and it hurts like crazy, but with all of you around me, I'll get through."

Megan held back the tears. She felt the same way. Jack would always be a part of their lives. His presence could be felt everywhere. All of his building projects were reminders of how much he did for them all.

To honor him, they had to keep going. Failure or giving up was not an option.

"Let's go learn how to play this game," Megan said grabbing her hand. "I have a feeling Linda and Rosie are going to be kicking our butts!"

They drank and laughed and enjoyed the camaraderie well into the night. For the first time in a long time, they could let down their guard and simply enjoy all the good in their lives.

Megan looked at Wyatt. His smile warmed her heart. She was

at peace. Right in this very moment, she was the happiest she had ever been in her life. She was going to cherish the moment. Megan knew it may not last forever.

End of 'Dark Defiance'

EMP Lodge Series Book Three

Thank You!

Thank you so much for purchasing and reading my book! My readers mean the world to me and without you I wouldn't be able to write these stories. If you enjoyed this book, please remember to leave a review on the book's Amazon page--I read every single one of them!

To be notified of my next release please sign up to my mailing list at www.GraceHamiltonBooks.com/mailing-list/

Grace Hamilton is the prepper pen-name for a bad-ass, survivalist momma-bear of four kids, and wife to a wonderful husband. After being stuck in a mountain cabin for six days following a flash flood, she decided she never wanted to feel so powerless or have to send her kids to bed hungry again. Now she lives the prepper lifestyle and knows that if SHTF or TEOTWAWKI happens, she'll be ready to help protect and provide for her family.

Combine this survivalist mentality with a vivid imagination (as well as a slightly unhealthy day dreaming habit) and you get a prepper fiction author. Grace spends her days thinking about the worst possible survival situations that a person could be thrown into, then throwing her characters into these nightmares while trying to figure out "What SHOULD you do in this situation?"

It's her wish that through her characters, you will get to experience what life will be like and essentially learn from their mistakes and experiences, so that you too can survive!

You can also follow Grace on Facebook at
fb.me/AuthorGraceHamilton

Sneak Peek

DARK
RETREAT

Blurb

Three months after life as she knows it was decimated, Megan Wolford has only one goal: protect her daughter, Caitlin, at any cost. When a mysterious illness strikes Caitlin down, Megan is forced to forage for medical supplies at a remote lodge. The last thing she wants is help from her fellow survivors when so many in her life have let her down—but soon she'll find herself with no other option.

Ex-Navy SEAL Wyatt Morris is doing everything he can to hold his family together after the tragic death of his prepper Dad, so when Megan enters their lands, he is mistrustful at first despite feeling drawn to her. He won't turn away an ill child though--no matter how deadly the world has become. But the arrival of another stranger named Kyle soon gives them all a new reason to be suspicious. Wyatt knows he'll have to forge alliances in order to keep his family safe, but trusting the wrong person could be a deadly mistake.

When Megan and Wyatt discover her daughter's illness may be linked to Kyle's arrival, it sets off a race to discover the truth before it's too late to save Caitlin—and the rest of the Morris clan. Can they work together for survival . . . and something more?

Get your copy of Dark Retreat at
GraceHamiltonBooks.com

Extract

Megan Wolford stumbled over a rock and nearly dropped her daughter before she quickly regained her footing. The sight of a log cabin through the trees had given her a boost of adrenaline and she found she was practically running through the damp forest despite her heavy burden.

She had fallen several times, bruising her knees and twisting her ankle. Her arms had deep cuts from tree branches that showed no mercy. There wasn't exactly a trail to follow, which meant she was cutting through the heart of the forest and its unforgiving terrain. She was making her own way, as usual, which always seemed to be far harder than it had to be.

"Caitlin, hold on, baby. Hold on," she whispered to the lifeless seven-year-old in her arms.

Megan was doing her best not to panic, but Caitlin had collapsed a couple miles back and she had been carrying the sleeping child ever since. Carrying her where she didn't know, but now that she saw what appeared to be a hunting lodge of some sort in front of her, she had a destination in mind. She had a goal.

It gave her something to focus on other than the agony that was tearing through her entire body. Another tree branch slapped her in the face, making her wince in pain. Her physical discomfort was nothing compared to the emotional anguish she felt at the thought of losing her daughter. Caitlin was the only thing she had left in this world. She couldn't lose her.

Her arms were burning and her lungs felt like they would collapse, but nothing would stop her from getting her daughter to what she hoped would be medicine. Without it, Megan knew her only child would die.

She didn't have a clue what had made her so sick, but Caitlin was gravely ill. In the past twenty-four hours, her daughter went from bubbly and energetic to lethargic and weak. Megan had left their most recent camp in the hopes of finding something to help her. They'd walked through one small town yesterday and found nothing. Every single place she checked had been emptied already forcing them to travel for miles.

She was afraid to walk through the city streets overrun with looters. Megan knew it wasn't safe for her and definitely not for Caitlin. It wasn't as if she could leave her daughter alone while she went on a scavenging mission. She had to do it with Caitlin or not all. Common sense told her she didn't have the strength to fight off the hundreds and thousands of other people vying for the same basic supplies. Instead, she had decided to head out of town in the hopes of finding clinics, stores, and homes in more rural areas that weren't as likely to be quite so dangerous.

1

Megan took long strides, slightly shifting her daughter, as she kept moving forward. Her sweaty hands were making it difficult for her to hold on to Caitlin. Gripping her hands together under her daughter's backside, Megan pressed on.

Get your copy of Dark Retreat at
GraceHamiltonBooks.com

Made in the USA
San Bernardino, CA
08 October 2017